WARRIORS
OF
VIRTUE

ROBERT TINE

BOULEVARD BOOKS, NEW YORK

WARRIORS OF VIRTUE

A Boulevard Book / published by arrangement with
IJL Creations, Inc. and Law Brothers Entertainment International, Ltd.

PRINTING HISTORY
Boulevard edition / May 1997

The Putnam Berkley World Wide Web site address is
http://www.berkley.com

ISBN: 1-57297-243-2

BOULEVARD
Boulevard Books are published by The Berkley Publishing Group,
200 Madison Avenue, New York, New York 10016.
BOULEVARD and its logo are trademarks
belonging to Berkley Publishing Corporation.

PRINTED IN THE UNITED STATES OF AMERICA

10 9 8 7 6 5 4 3 2 1

Acknowledgments

Many thanks to Christopher Law for all his tireless work on the novel's behalf.

WARRIORS
OF
VIRTUE

1

It could have been any town anywhere in the country, a perfect, picture-postcard slice of suburban America: a typical middle-class neighborhood made up of modest homes on well-kept lawns, station wagons and minivans parked in almost every driveway. It was a warm, sunny Southern California Saturday morning and the weekend routine had been substituted for the habits of the workweek. Lawnmowers muttered throughout the neighborhood, a teenager or two worked in driveways washing cherished cars, people lounged in backyards, enjoying an extra cup of coffee and a little longer with the morning paper than they allowed themselves on the other days of the week.

None of this was true, however, for the Jeffers household. Kathryn Jeffers was a real estate agent and Saturdays and Sundays were the busiest days of her workweek. Added to that, her husband was out of town—that meant another long, parentless day for her twelve-year-old son, Ryan. Kathryn felt guilty about that—but she knew she would feel even guiltier if she was not bringing in the money she made at her job. She shrugged off her guilt as best she could, telling herself that two-income families were just a fact of life these days.

Kathryn Jeffers checked the breakfast she had laid out on the kitchen table—a steaming plate of scrambled eggs, a couple of strips of bacon, a pile of toast and a tall glass of orange juice—then turned her attentions to her bulging briefcase.

"Ryan! Breakfast is on the table! Come on now!" Kathryn stuffed catalogues and papers into the attaché case, but there were far too many of them.

From somewhere deep in the house came an answer of sorts. "Okay . . ." Her son sounded preoccupied, distracted. It was not an out of the ordinary reaction from him these days, something Kathryn Jeffers put down to "a phase."

"I've got to run," Kathryn shouted. "I'll be

home around five. Okay?" She waited a few moments. "Okay, Ryan?" she repeated.

She waited a few moments longer. Finally: "'Kay . . . Bye."

"Good-bye, honey." Kathryn picked up the briefcase with one hand and scooped up an armful of catalogues with the other. Before leaving the kitchen, she checked her appearance in the mirror—she was a pretty woman in her mid-thirties, with a short pageboy haircut, sparkling blue eyes and glasses that perched on the end of her nose. Kathryn shrugged to herself—she couldn't change the way she looked—and bustled out of the kitchen, hooking the door closed with her foot.

Her car—actually, an oversized four-wheel-drive Jeep with cell phone, fax and laptop computer, as well as a change of clothes, cosmetics and a ton of reference books and catalogues, which served as an office and studio apartment on wheels—was parked in the driveway but, with her hands full, opening the door on the driver's side presented something of a problem. She reached with the hand full of the catalogues, but succeeded only in dropping all of them. The booklets slithered out of her arm and scattered on the asphalt of the driveway.

"Shoot!" she said. As she knelt to pick them up, Ryan's dog, Bravo, a good-natured bear of a golden retriever, came bounding out of nowhere and thrust his wet nose into her face. Bravo liked nothing more than interacting with humans—particularly members of his immediate family, the Jeffers. He figured that if Kathryn was so close to the ground—his turf, literally—then she must want to play. He bounced and capered and barked a little, trying to figure out what game it was she wanted to play, and when she didn't give any clear sign, he moved in close to lick her face again, just to get her in the mood for some fun.

"Bravo! No! Get away from me, you dumb dog!" Kathryn did her best to fight him off and get the catalogues at the same time.

"Bravo! No!" She tried to push the dog's soft muzzle away. "Look, I have to tell you—dog spit I don't need." Then she pointed over her shoulder, back toward the Jeffers house. "Where's Ryan, Bravo? Go on, boy. Go find Ryan. Make sure he eats his breakfast for once. Instead of you eating his breakfast for him."

Bravo looked at her with sweet, gentle but thoroughly uncomprehending eyes. He was not the smartest canine on earth but even he had sort of figured out that Kathryn was not in the mood to play just then. Bravo whimpered a little and backed up, watching as she gathered up her papers, opened the door of the car and swept a pile of "For Sale" lawn signs off the back seat.

"Go on. Ask him to take you to that game of

his," she said. That was another thing she felt guilty about. Because of her weekend work schedule she almost never managed to make it to one of the junior high football games. If Kathryn could be sure of two things about her son, one of them was this: he was fascinated by the martial arts. Karate, Kung Fu, Judo, Jujitsu—she wasn't really sure which one he was so devoted to. In her "Mom's mind" they were all more or less the same, weren't they? Whichever one it was— maybe it was all of them—Ryan's room was a riot of magazines, books and posters all devoted to the study and practice of Eastern techniques of self-defense.

The space not devoted to the martial arts was given over to her son's other obsession: football. Ryan was football crazy. During the season Ryan never seemed to miss a college game on Saturdays or a pro game on Sundays. Monday nights, of course, were sacred. When the bowl games were played at the end of the college season, Ryan had to be surgically removed from the couch in front of the television set. Superbowl Sunday itself was something more akin to a religious experience than a sporting event.

In addition to the pleasures of televised football, Ryan was involved in the sport in a practical manner as well. He was an integral part of the squad at his junior high school. At least Kathryn liked to think of her son as being essential to the team's continual success. It wasn't that he was a player, though—he was not the star quarterback, the fast, graceful receiver or even a defense man who stood between the other team and victory like a tall, wide slab of beef, impervious to pain. Ryan (along with his best friend Chucky) was the all-important water and towel boy for the team, although his official title was "assistant equipment manager." It was better than nothing.

Ryan was slight and had been a delicate child growing up. It seemed that his early years had been one health crisis after another, and the childhood ailments and diseases that other kids went through without noticeable difficulty always seemed to hit Ryan hard. The measles, which other kids recovered from in a week, had laid poor Ryan low for twenty-one days. Mumps had taken even longer to shake, as had the chicken pox. But those days were gone, consigned to the ages six to eight . . .

Ryan's real problems had come at birth and no one knew anything about them until it was too late to do much. Ryan had begun to walk right when he was supposed to—around eighteen months—but it was not until he was two that anyone noticed he had a slightly odd gait and was prone to falling down even more than toddlers tended to do. A pediatric orthopedic surgeon had discovered that an intrauterine event had caused devastating damage to the neurologic development of his right leg. A series of operations was recommended, but the results, after eleven terrible weeks with Ryan in a cast that enveloped his little body, were found wanting. The left leg had turned out fine, but the right leg was still crippled and weak. That led to the ugly leather-and-steel leg brace he had to wear from time to time—and a terminal case of the guilts as far as Kathryn and her husband were concerned.

As Ryan grew older and developed his all-consuming interest in sports, it became apparent that he would never play them. Kathryn wondered if her son had chosen to get interested in the most physical of sports because he was slightly disabled, rather than turning his back on something that he would be denied direct involvement in forever.

She knew the limp and the brace bothered Ryan. As far as she knew he had never been teased about either. Still, it was no secret that kids of Ryan's age, particularly the hulking, cocky football jocks, could be as cruel as a bunch of preadolescent Marquis de Sades.

Kathryn was just about to start the engine when she felt a profound, sharp twinge of guilt. She sighed to herself, opened the car door and walked back to the house. She opened the front door a crack and called out.

"Ryan?"

"Yeah?" he answered. Her son was still se-

7

creted somewhere deep in the house, apparently not having moved since she left. Breakfast, no doubt, was right where she'd left it on the table.

"Have a good game, okay?" she called. "I love you!"

"Okay." Right at that moment, Ryan did not sound as if he really cared all that much . . . Kathryn sighed again and retraced her footsteps out of the house to her car. Ryan was all right, she said to herself. He was just fine. It was just that he was a kid. And kids, it was well known, were extremely difficult to figure out in any meaningful way. Still, there was no way Kathryn could ever quite escape that gnawing sense of guilt that always seemed to travel with her, the sense that somehow she had failed her only child.

Bravo watched as Kathryn backed the car out of the driveway, then he turned and trotted back to the house. Bravo may not have been the most intelligent of dogs, but he knew how a few things worked—like the ease of getting through the front door of a suburban house. It was all in the nose—Bravo poked his long snout into the crack where the door met the frame, with just enough force to unlatch it, opening up the front door. Then he wiggled his wide body through the crack he'd made and vanished into the house. The dog padded through the entrance hall, pausing in the kitchen just long enough to snatch a piece of toast from the plate on the breakfast table, then moving on swiftly down the hallway to the rear, where the bedrooms were.

There was a good reason for Ryan's preoccupation, for his distance, for his general lack of interest in anything his mother said to him that morning. Ryan was reading. He was so deeply engrossed in his reading that nothing else could penetrate his mind—the world around him receded. He had forgotten what day it was (Saturday) or where he was (bathroom—more precisely, actually *on* the toilet).

He wasn't reading about football, not this time. Rather, the boy was engrossed in the other of his obsessions—the martial arts. It took a long time for Ryan to realize that he was being watched. Reluctantly, he tore his eyes from the page of his comic book and looked up to find Bravo standing right in front of him, the piece of toast still in his mouth, patiently waiting for Ryan to react.

Ryan looked down at his comic book again. "Bravo, do you mind?" he said, instantly engrossed in his comic book again. The comic book was far more interesting than any dog, even a dog bearing breakfast, and Ryan's eyes raced through its brightly colored panels. The drawings were extravagant, enchanting, slightly fanciful scenes, the story of Kung Fu masters battling to the death in a classic struggle of good versus evil. His mother may not have been able to tell

Karate from a bunch of carrots, Judo from Sumo wrestling or Kung Fu from King Kong, but the distinctions for Ryan were as plain as black and white. He was not interested in the first two, not at all. It was Kung Fu that enchanted him, the grace of the movements as well as the emphasis that the discipline put on the importance of right versus wrong and the belief that the morally upright and virtuous would always triumph over the base, corrupt and evil, no matter how great the differences in power. It was comforting for a twelve-year-old to be told that the good guys always win, no matter how hopeless the situation might appear, no matter how desperate the fight or the numbers of enemies ranged against you. The truth of it was—Ryan didn't have too many friends, and if he could tell himself that he was always on the side of truth and right and justice, then he would be able to get through his days with his dignity and self-respect more or less intact. At least he hoped it worked that way.

Right then, though, he was in the middle of a pretty exciting battle to the death and he really did not want to be disturbed. Not by his mother—and certainly not by his dog and something as completely mundane and boring as breakfast.

Bravo did not see things that way, of course—he had been given his orders and he was going to do his best to carry them out. He watched his young master for a few more moments and then with obvious canine disdain dropped the toast in the middle of the comic book.

That did it. The deposit of a slightly drool-sodden slice of toast smack-dab in the middle of the story broke the spell. Ryan groaned, swept away the bread and the crumbs and realized it was time to say good-bye to the struggle of absolute good versus unmitigated evil and turn himself to the more trying task of getting through the day . . .

IMAGINE THE HOTTEST, MOST HUMID SUMMER DAY, ADD THE noise in the engine room of an old tramp steamer, plus the crush and the crowd of a commuter train at rush hour—put it all together and you have a fair idea of what the kitchen is like in the typical Chinese restaurant.

Cramped, hot and steamy, the kitchen of the Golden River Noodle Company was jammed with a dozen cooks toiling over two dozen woks, deep vats filled with of sizzling oil, the food dancing and crackling in the heat. Steam, smoke and the occasional small ball of flame filled the air, and the slap and clatter of spatulas and ladles on blackened steel rang out like so much sword-play.

It was not the kind of place you'd expect to find a twelve-year-old kid hanging out, but everyone in school thought that there was something a little strange about Ryan Jeffers. Not weird strange . . . It was more that he seemed to have his own, highly individual view of the world, his own specialized set of likes and dislikes. And one of them happened to be tucking himself into the corner of the kitchen at the Golden River Noodle Company and watching the action. And the food was good too.

The kitchen seemed to go day and night like a blast furnace—people wanted Chinese food at the most peculiar times and it seemed to be of the utmost importance to the Golden River staff that they get it *now*. To add to the confusion, everyone seemed to be talking at once, and loudly too. The cooks bellowed at the assistants, who yelled right back. The waiters and waitresses stormed into the kitchen as if attacking it, yelled out orders for the cashiers and curses at the cooks for not being fast enough with the food. No one seemed to like anyone else—and there were *real* intense likes and dislikes from time to time, although these were rare. The first time Ryan squeezed into the kitchen, he had expected physical fights to break out among the cooks or between the waiters and the cooks every five minutes. Of course, it never happened. Still, it looked and sounded like a barely contained riot.

In a corner were the two cashiers, two women bent over two cash registers, telephones permanently attached to their ears, their fingers flying over the keys, keeping track of every transaction like recording angels. Two other phones rang constantly.

The first time Ryan Jeffers had seen the kitchen of the Golden River he had been amazed that anything—let alone complex and delicious meals—came out of such confusion and chaos. It did not seem possible that those hot, toiling cooks and snarling waiters could possibly be communicating or that the cashiers could cut through all the noise and tumult to remember to record that table six had ordered a double order of brown rice. The pandemonium of that kitchen was certainly entertaining to twelve-year-old Ryan, and he tried to stop in for a visit whenever he could, but each time he returned he was amazed that the place was still in business.

Gradually, though, Ryan began to notice that what appeared to be a riot in a kitchen was, in fact, a carefully ordered system which turned out meals with the efficiency of an assembly line. Each person in that narrow room had a job to do, tasks to be performed over and over again, each employee a cog in a machine that worked perfectly. That the cooks tended to shout at one another throughout the day was more tradition than anything else, as was the eternal rivalry between the cook staff and the waiters. None of the cooks seemed to think it strange that a twelve-year-old "round eye" boy would want to spend part of his afternoons watching them cook. They were, after all, masters of their craft and deserved to be observed as they went about their tasks.

A man named Ming was Ryan's friend and favorite cook. Ming had been the first to invite Ryan into the kitchen, when he had seen him peering through the double swinging doors trying to catch a glimpse of the cooks every time one door or the other swung open and a waiter came barreling out.

Ryan was shy at first, but Ming had coaxed him in, placed him in the corner out of the way and given him a bowl of noodles and a rimless cup of tea, telling him to enjoy the show.

It was impossible to tell how old Ming was—he could have been forty or seventy or even older—but he moved like an athlete, wielding his spatula and his chef's knife with the grace of a fencer. Through his knowledge of football and his love of the martial arts, Ryan knew a graceful performance when he saw it—never mind if this man happened to be a cook, rather than a running back or Kung Fu warrior.

As far as Ryan could tell, Ming never stopped moving. An assistant constantly fed him vegetables and meat chopped and diced, sliding them down the counter to where Ming took over, deftly flipping a pile of diced carrots or a tangled knot of noodles into a wok, stir-frying for a moment or two, adding salt and sauce in a blur, controlling everything with no more than a flick of the wrist or a wave of the spatula.

That day Ryan sat on a counter behind Ming, a bowl of rice in his hands, watching every movement with the fascination of the devoted fan. It was like observing a skilled martial artist going through his moves. As fast as a machine, Ming chopped some chicken into thin ribbons of white meat, mixed it with some silver-and-gold strands of egg, then added rice. Then the entire mixture went into a hot wok, where he seared it for a moment or two. Ming picked up the long wooden handle of the wok and flipped the pot, throwing the food high into the air—then he whirled, grabbed another pan and caught the mixture in it on the way down. Ryan laughed and felt he should applaud.

Ming looked over his shoulder and winked at Ryan. "Hold out the bowl," he said.

Ryan did as he was told, extending his arms and holding the small rice bowl out over the floor of the kitchen. Ming glanced over his shoulder.

"No," he said. "Hold it a little to your right."

"Okay," said Ryan, doing as he was told. He had no idea what was going to happen next, but he had a feeling whatever it was was going to be something of a showstopper.

"Now," said Ming. "Watch closely."

The leading edge of Ming's stainless-steel

spatula sliced into a pile of white rice steaming in a cooker, and without even looking at Ryan's bowl, he flipped the rice over his shoulder, the white, sticky clump sailing through the air and landing with a faint plop in Ryan's dish.

He laughed and shook his head. "Good shot, Ming," he said. "Really good shot. *Almost* as cool as Kung Fu."

Ming winked. "Almost as cool as Kung Fu? No, no, no, this is beyond Kung Fu, Ryan." Without warning, Ming whipped around and Ryan saw something blurry fly from the cook's hands. Ryan looked down into his rice bowl and saw that two chopsticks were embedded in the rice, quivering slightly like arrows.

Ryan laughed again. "Well, its certainly different," he said. Ryan gripped his chopsticks awkwardly, but did manage to transfer some rice from the bowl to his mouth without dropping too much on the floor of the kitchen. His handling of the chopsticks could use some work, but he was determined to get the hang of it. He had the distinct feeling that Ming and the rest of the cooks had pretty low opinions of the "round eyes" who desecrated their food creations with the use of the barbaric knife and fork. Ryan was determined that he would not incur their silent disdain.

"No, no," said Ming, vehemently, looking hard at Ryan. "Real Kung Fu. The arts of the Kung Fu masters, the real thing. The real masters of Kung Fu had their strength, not in weapons, but in *here!*"

He flipped the spatula high in the air, caught the business end of it in his right hand and tapped the center of his chest with the handle. Then he launched the spatula over his shoulder, reached behind him, and caught the utensil on its way down. "Understand?"

Ryan nodded, but he wasn't really all that sure what Ming was talking about. "I guess . . . You mean, you gotta have heart? Something like that, Ming?"

Ming laughed. "Yeah, something like that . . . Heart and mind are weapons too," Ming explained. "They are the weapons of the old Kung Fu masters. Weapons mean nothing without heart, Ryan. You should have learned that by now."

"They are?" said Ryan. "I should have?" He shoveled a little rice into his mouth and dropped almost none of it. One of these days he would definitely get the hang of the chopsticks.

Ming nodded. "Have I ever told you about the true masters of Kung Fu, Ryan?"

Ryan shook his head. "Nope. I didn't really know that you . . . I didn't know you *knew* the secrets of the Kung Fu masters, Ming. I didn't know you knew any Kung Fu masters at all, let alone their secrets."

Ming leaned closer, as if about to impart a

17

great secret. "Then let go of your limitations, Ryan, and try to imagine a different world beyond anything you've ever seen."

Ryan looked more than a little puzzled by Ming's enigmatic words. "What do you mean?"

"Imagine a perfect world," said Ming with a slow smile. "A world with no worries. A world of perfect bliss. A world where anything can happen." He leaned in even closer and lowered his voice to almost a whisper. "You think a world like that cannot exist? You think I'm making it up?" Ming looked down at Ryan critically, as if to say "Oh ye of little faith," or at least the Chinese version of the phrase.

"I . . . I don't know," Ryan stammered. "I don't know. *Are* you making it up, Ming?"

The cook shook his head slowly. "This world can exist, Ryan. It needs only one thing."

"What?" Ryan asked. "What does it need?"

"It needs great warriors to defend it," said Ming portentously. "A world like that must be defended by the greatest warriors. Warriors who are not only strong and graceful, but good. Their hearts are pure. Without that, they could never be great enough."

Ryan's eyes were wide and he could feel a tremor of excitement as he grappled to imagine the world Ming described. The way he spoke it seemed to Ryan that this world actually existed

18

somewhere, but that entrance was restricted to the chosen few.

Ming pivoted on one heel and kicked the burner switch on the huge gas range, and flame erupted under one of the woks. He flung a mixture of vegetables—carrots, scallions, bean sprouts—along with a handful of ropy noodles into the wok, and hot steam gushed into the air.

Ryan was as taken with the performance of the cook as he had been with the comic book characters. Suddenly all the noise in the riotous kitchen seemed to lessen, as if someone had hit a Mute button, and Ryan focused on Ming, his graceful movements and his enchanting words.

"No guns, no lasers, no morphing," said Ming. "They used the forces of nature as their weapons. The force of *fire!*"

Ming hit the oil spigot over the wok, and as soon as the liquid hit the hot metal, a great sheet of hot flame erupted and then died down almost immediately.

"And *metal!*" The cook grabbed a huge, short-handled Chinese cleaver and chopped a skein of purple-pink octopus tentacles into tiny pieces. It happened so fast that Ryan didn't see Ming's hand at all, the cleaver was nothing more than a silver blur. One moment the octopus was whole, the next it was in perfect pieces, all exactly the same size.

"And *water!*" He plunged a ladle into a pot of

cold water, then threw the water into the wok, and another burst of steam and heat erupted. The pieces of octopus were dumped into the pot and with hardly a pause Ming continued to work at the magnificent dish.

"They were warriors, Ryan! Warriors who fought for integrity and honor. They could sail upon their enemies with the grace of a dancer. They could knock them senseless with the touch of a feather. Can you imagine such a thing as that, Ryan?"

It was all Ryan could do to get his voice to work, so taken was he with Ming's vision. "No . . . no . . ."

"Well, you should believe," the cook ordered. "It is a good thing to believe."

Ming was flinging and tossing pieces of octopus and vegetables all over the place, his movements becoming wild—but somehow, oddly enough, controlled at the same time. Steam and smoke filled the cramped room, building to a crescendo, like a volcano on the verge of eruption.

Then, it was all over. Ming grabbed a large serving plate and dumped the octopus, noodle and vegetable creation onto the dish. It was a vertical, almost architectural, pile of food, a woven delight of fish, octopus, vegetables and noodles glistening under a sheen of hot, fragrant oil. Curls of smoke danced around the food.

"Wow," said Ryan, staring at the serving plate. "That is beautiful, Ming. Really cool."

"Tastes good too," said Ming with a wink.

A waiter snarled something in Cantonese, pushed between Ryan and Ming and grabbed the dish Ming had just created.

"Finally!" he said in English. "Finally you finish with that thing! I got guests starving here."

"Take it," said Ming with a shrug.

The magic and magnificent world seemed to recede and the sounds and heat of the kitchen came flooding back into the room.

The cook next to Ming on the line, a surly old man named Lang, glanced at his neighbor and frowned at Ryan Jeffers.

"Ha!" he said. "While you show off, the customers starve." He waved a spatula at Ryan. "And there is no room in here for him . . . *master*." Lang then returned to his native language and let out a stream of words that Ryan had no doubt would have been a little tough on his young years. Then Lang laughed to himself, cackling harshly, as if he thought that he had put Ming in his place, and big-time at that.

Ming did not answer the old man directly. Rather, the fire and the fight seemed to have gone out of him. All he did was push Ryan a little farther into the corner, to get him out of the way of the cooks and waiters.

Then he sighed deeply. "It is nice to talk of the

great virtuous warriors, Ryan. But now it is time for more cooking, I think. Back to work."

Ming turned and hit an old lever set in the wall, the handle worn smooth by years of use. High above their heads a skylight swung open with a thud. All of a sudden, the heat and the steam vanished, replaced by cool, sweet, fresh air, and light poured into the dimly lit kitchen.

The loss of his carefully constructed octopus dish did not seem to bother Ming all that much— he was used to it and in time he knew he would make another. He turned a faucet above his wok, filling the pan with a stream of cold water, sending another cloud of steam into the air.

Ryan knew that he should leave and let his friend get on with his work, but the words had inflamed him. His head buzzed with questions and he needed answers.

"The Kung Fu masters," said Ryan tentatively. "Do they still exist? Are they still around today?"

Ming worked his spatula around the inside of the wok, scoring away any bits of burnt food, but was careful not to scrape through the smooth patina on the steel. He looked at Ryan, saw the intensity in the boy's eyes and tried not to laugh. "Do they exist? Of course!"

Ryan's eyes grew wide and he leaned closer. "They do? Where? Where are they?"

Ming looked over his shoulder, smirked and winked. "Oh, Ryan . . . I can't tell you that."

Ryan looked disappointed. "Why not?"

Ming winked again, but this time he broke out into a full-fledged grin. "*Ancient Chinese secret* . . . Ryan."

Ryan sighed and looked a little disappointed. Maybe an ancient Chinese secret would help him solve some of his more immediate problems. The alarm on his wristwatch beeped.

"I've gotta bail, Ming," he said. "I gotta get going or I'm going to be late for my game."

"Okay, Ryan," said Ming. He poured a thin stream of oil into the wok and set it on the ring above the dancing blue gas flame. He was ready to start cooking again. "Okay . . . Next time you come, I tell you some more stories. How about that?"

"Cool," said Ryan. "And thanks for lunch."

Lang looked over at him. "Leaving already?" he said sourly. "Maybe you stay for dinner too."

"I wish I could. Bye all," said Ryan. He spun his rice bowl on the counter in front of Lang and then scooted out of the room. Lang watched him go, then turned back to his cooking.

"No respect," he said with disgust.

2

IT WAS SECOND AND TEN, HARDLY ANY TIME ON THE CLOCK.
The score: home 16, visitors 20. It didn't matter if
it was the Rose Bowl, the Super Bowl or just a
game played between two junior high school
teams in the Valley like this one. There was no
more tense situation in sports than this. A few
yards away was the goal line. The distance was
not great; you could stroll it in a few seconds. In
a football game it might as well be a mile or
more.

Ryan Jeffers could feel the pent-up anxiety of
the crowd—a bleacher filled with anxious moms,
dads and students—worry radiating off them

like heat. And he could feel his own heart beating a mile a minute too, as if it was going to break out of his thin chest. He stood in a crowd of players, the defensive players who had done all they could. Now all they could do was watch. Ryan was there on the sidelines telling himself not to watch, but unable to stop himself from watching. He glanced up at the scoreboard and looked at the clock, as if maybe he had misread it the last time he looked. Nope. It was just the same. Just a few seconds stood between victory and defeat— a period of time that could pass in a moment or last an eternity.

Standing next Ryan was his friend Chucky. Chucky had his hands over his eyes. "I can't watch," Chucky muttered. "Ryan, tell me when its over. Okay? If we lose, kill me quick, okay?"

Ryan paid no attention. "Come on, come on . . . ," he whispered urgently. "Thirty seconds. You can do it, Brad." Brad was the quarterback. Ryan did not like him, but he knew he could play this game. If anyone was going to control the ball in a tense situation like this it would be Brad.

The two teams set up on the opposition's forty-yard line, the end zone as wide and as green as a suburban lawn—but it seemed like it was a mile away. Suddenly, the defensive line of the opposing team looked like a solid rank of giants, each one seeming to grow a foot as Ryan watched. It was at moments like these that the other side always looked unbeatable.

He could hear Brad, the quarterback, calling the audibles, then he saw the center snap the ball. Then everything seemed to slow down, as if each second was now a minute, maybe two minutes long. The defense surged forward and the home team seemed to splinter under the assault, but they slowed the attack down long enough for the quarterback to drop back and roll out of the pocket and, dodging a tackler, set and fire the ball. Then, it looked as if he changed his mind, passing the ball off to a running back. The back broke one tackle and charged but was brought down by a tackler on the fifteen-yard line.

Chucky had been watching. He couldn't help himself. "Ah man," he said sadly. "That's it. We're terminated."

It seemed to Ryan as if the whole team organization had broken down. The play was over but the clock hadn't stopped because the running back hadn't made it out of bounds. The coach was fumbling through the playbook, looking for some strategy that would save the day, the players on the field looking over, waiting for some kind of direction.

"Hey," said Ryan. "Come on! The clock is ticking!"

The coach glanced at the clock and blanched. "Time out!" he yelled. "Time out!"

The referee blew his whistle and the coach wiped his brow nervously. He looked over at his water boys, angry and impatient. "Ryan? Chucky? *Today, please?*"

"Oh," said Chucky.

"Right," said Ryan.

The two of them fell in behind the coach as he trotted out to his players. They passed around the water bottles as the coach tried to rally his troops. Ryan's leg had been bothering him a little and his mother insisted that he wear his leather-and-steel brace. He hated wearing it, of course, but it wasn't like no one had seen it before. Everyone in the whole school knew he limped. Most of the time kids were pretty cool about it, but sometimes, some of them . . . Ryan shook off the thought and made for the field.

As always, he felt a little out of place among athletes, but he faced his disability square on by taking any job he could get on the football squad. If this was the best he could do, then he would take it and do his best to be the best at his job. Making friends with Chucky had been an added benefit. Together, they got each other through every game.

The coach edged into the huddle, looking like a man who had reached the outer edge of his leadership abilities. Brad, the cocky quarterback, seemed to sneer slightly as the man spoke, as if he knew the game of football better than any coach. Ryan, however, was listening closely to the coache's words, analyzing them, thinking the way Brad should have been but wasn't.

"Okay, listen up." The coach looked from face to face. "We've got time for one play." He licked his lips nervously. "Sweep left . . . no, sweep *right*. And Toby gets the ball. Got it?"

"No way, Coach," said Brad indignantly. "That left tackle has been busting through the line for the whole game."

"Hey," said the coach sourly. "I've played a few games, son, okay? I said sweep right, so sweep right. Now, let's go." He slapped his hands together and walked quickly from the field, as if he just wanted to get this game over and done with.

Brad looked disgusted, then put his hand out to Ryan for a water bottle. He actually smiled at Ryan as he took it.

"Thanks," said Brad. He put the bottle to his lips and took a long swig of the cold water.

Ryan swallowed deep and somehow found the courage to speak. "Um, Brad . . ." Ryan wasn't sure that his voice could be heard above the roaring of the crowd.

Brad took the bottle from his lips. "Yeah?" Then he started to drink again.

"Their, um, right safety comes inside on every play," Ryan said, gaining confidence with every word. He knew his football, even if his defective leg wouldn't allow him to play the game. "If you fake to Toby, then bootleg left, you'll have a clear path to the end zone."

Brad stopped in the middle of the drink and stared down at Ryan, the look on his face suggesting amazement, as if a monkey had suddenly started to talk to him. Then Ryan noticed that all of the other players on the offensive squad were looking at him with the same look—an unpleasant mixture of astonishment and repugnance.

"Look," said Ryan desperately, "I've been watching this game. I've been watching him and—"

Brad took the bottle away from his lips and spat a long stream of water on Ryan's shoe, then tossed the bottle to him. "Here," he said. "Now, get lost." Brad turned back to the game. Ryan had the distinct impression that the cocky quarterback had already forgotten that he even existed.

Mortified, Ryan hurried off the field as fast as he could, following Chucky to the sidelines. As the reached the edge of the field, Ryan looked into the stands and saw a young girl, Tracy—the prettiest girl in the school—and she was smiling at him. Ryan immediately felt a little better. It was as if somehow she alone had figured out that he was trying his best, giving everything he could for the good of the team. Ryan smiled back and felt a little better—until he realized that she was looking right past him. As he watched, Tracy threw her arms in the air and shouted at the top of her lungs.

"Go, Brad!"

Ryan did his best to shrug off the hurt and embarrassment. "Figures," he muttered under his breath. The way the universe was ordered—in junior high school at any rate—the quarterback always got the best looking girl in the school. It was like the school district or the principal or something *assigned* them to each other at the beginning of the year.

On the field the two lines had formed up and Brad called for the snap. Toby was in motion as the quarterback took the ball from the center, but as he looked for his receiver he saw the right safety charging in—just as Ryan said he would. Toby swept by, his arms out for the ball, but Brad didn't hand off as he had been instructed to do.

Ryan heard the coach yelling at the top of his lungs as he watched his desperation play collapse almost as soon as it got started. "What's he doing?" he bellowed. "What the hell is that kid doing?"

The defense line was swarming toward Toby, paying no attention to Brad, who doglegged left and then dug in his heels and burned up the field toward the end zone. The clock had ticked down to zero, but the play was still alive. Two defensemen, then a third, realized that Toby didn't have the ball and tore off after Brad. The lumbering runners bore down on him like a squad of armored tanks but the quarterback scampered away from the three diving tackles and charged into the end zone.

Ryan could have sworn that for a full second there was complete silence in the stands and on the field—then the entire place went berserk. The crowd in the stands erupted, their tension swept away by relief and rapture: they screamed, they hollered, they hugged and danced.

On the sidelines where Ryan stood, the defensive players stormed onto the field, pushing aside lesser mortals like the water boy and the equipment manager to race out to their fellow players. Ryan, picking himself up from the churned-up turf, looked at the celebration on the field and felt a genuine excitement at the hard-won victory, but somewhere inside he did not really feel like it was his to share, as if he was *really* part of the team.

After all, he wasn't an active player or even a reserve. He wasn't a player at all—he was only the lowly and much put-down equipment manager. Never mind that it had been his play. There was no way he would ever assign himself the credit for the win. And if he knew football players the way he thought he did, no one would ever know.

Ryan dusted himself off and then hurried out

onto the field to join in the celebration. If anyone had been watching him, the reason he was not a player would have been plain—there was a hesitancy in his step, a distinct limp that slowed him down, a limp that—this being junior high school, after all—set him ever so slightly apart . . .

Only Chucky knew what was going on. He clapped Ryan on the back. "Nice call, Ry," he said. "If it hadn't been for you, all those heroes out there would be walking back to the showers banging their helmets and putting together their excuses."

"Yeah . . . Well, what difference does it make?" Ryan replied, looking down. "We won, didn't we?"

THE CELEBRATION CONTINUED IN THE LOCKER ROOM. Coach Turner went from player to player patting them on the back saying the same thing over and over again: "Heck of a game, boys. That's the way to handle 'em." As if he had been the one who had originated the play that had won the game.

Ryan followed in his wake, almost smothered under the pile of clean towels he carried, handing them out one by one, a compliment going along with each one of them.

"Here you go, Ted," Ryan said to Ted, the hulking linebacker who was the cornerstone of the team's defense. Despite his strength and his skills on the field, Ted was modest and easy-going, leaving the arrogance and strutting to the quarterback and his clique.

Ted took the towel. "Thanks, buddy. Good game, huh, Ryan? What'd you think? Did we show 'em, or what?"

"Man," said Ryan, his voice filled with admiration. "You knocked Stenson so far off the ball he never knew what hit him. I think he's going to be bruised for a week."

Ted laughed and nodded vigorously. "Tell me about it! You should have heard him trying to catch his breath."

Ryan worked his way down the line of lockers handing out his towels, his limp evident—it always got a little more pronounced when he had been standing for a long time and at that point he had been on his feet for hours. Still, he put it out his mind and did his job.

He had a joke or a compliment for every member of the team and each one responded in kind, all of them laughing, delighted with their victory, sharing in the joy of *the team*, a unit functioning together, no matter if one's role was on the field or off of it.

The last six athletes Ryan approached, however, did not seem to share in the concept of team work. They kept to themselves in a corner of the locker room, segregated from the others, not even joining in the general celebration. They sat on the benches in front of their lockers, still dressed in their mud- and sweat-stained jerseys, talking low and sniggering among themselves. These were the arrogant jocks, the circle centered on Brad, the classic strutting junior high school quarterback, and his primary sidekick, Toby, the typical arrogant running back. That they were both skilled players was beyond a shadow of a doubt. It was their general performance as human beings that left something—a lot, really—to be desired.

Ryan hesitated a moment before approaching them—but only for a moment or two, figuring that in the aftermath of a hard-fought win even these conceited jocks would show a little human warmth. It would only be natural, wouldn't it?

"Hey, Brad," said Ryan. "That was a great game, really great." He shook his head as if he couldn't think of words sufficient to describe Brad's prowess on the football field. Ryan was still naive enough to think that Brad might, *just might*, acknowledge the debt he owed him. But Ryan was to be disappointed.

Brad looked at Ryan coldly, as if he was a general who had unexpectedly been addressed by a lowly private. "Got a towel, Jeffers?"

Ryan nodded. "Yeah."

Brad thrust out a hand and his face twisted into a disdainful sneer. *"Then hand it over,"* he said spitefully. It had never dawned on Ryan that the pivotal role he had played in gaining Brad the ground on the field, and the glory off of it, would make the quarterback all the more arrogant. Brad knew, if no one else did, that if it hadn't been for lowly Ryan Jeffers, he would have been humiliated in front of the entire school. Brad hid it but he knew, inside, that he was in Ryan's debt.

"Yeah, right," Ryan said diffidently, his eyes down. He passed the towel to Brad, who snapped it away. The other five grabbed their towels from him roughly, then Ryan turned to walk away.

"Hey, Jeffers . . ." This was Toby, taking his cue from Brad. Ryan turned back.

"Yeah?"

"You still want to be a Buddy?"

Ryan thought: *Doesn't everybody?* And he almost said it too, but he knew that would not be cool. To be a Buddy was to be accepted, to be part of the elite, a sort of junior high school secret society that automatically conferred respect on members. Any member of the football team was in the club by a sort of junior high school divine right. Needless to say, that right did not extend to the equipment manager—guys like Ryan had to earn their way in. And they almost never got the chance.

In his heart of hearts, deep down, Ryan knew that being a Buddy was basically bull, but in the black-and-white world of junior high school he thought that his problems would be solved if only he could make it into the elite circle, a validation he could use like a lucky charm.

"Hey," said Toby. "I asked you a question. I asked if you still wanna be a Buddy."

Ryan nodded slowly. "Yeah," he said. "I guess . . ."

Brad took over. He smirked and took a step closer to Ryan. He spun his sweaty jockstrap around his index finger. "Well, you know . . . If you *really* want to be a buddy, you have to be initiated, right?"

"I dunno," said Ryan hesitantly. The word initiation always carried with it unpleasant connotations.

Brad ignored Ryan's reluctance. "Step one." He glanced over his shoulder and leered at his cronies, then looked back at Ryan. "Put this around your face." Quickly, he pushed the sweaty, stained athletic supporter under Ryan's nose.

The cronies did their best to stifle their laughter—their faces went red and they snorted like bulls—but before Ryan could react, Coach Turner stepped in and swiped the jock out of Brad's hand.

"Hey, Brad. Cut it out and hit the shower," Coach Turner ordered. "Nobody here has any interest in seeing you wave your jock around, okay? Got it?"

"Aww, Coach, c'mon . . . ," said Brad. "We were just fooling around. Right, Ryan?"

"That's right," Ryan mumbled. He hated himself for backing up Brad, but he knew that to tell the truth was to make himself dead—or worse. Brad and the Buddies could, if they chose, make his life a living hell instead of the mildly unpleasant experience it was now.

"See, Coach," said Toby. "No harm done. We we're just messing around. That's all."

Coach Turner put his hands on his hips and glared at Brad and his gang. He looked unimpressed, not to mention unconvinced. He had grown up in locker rooms, spent his whole life in them. He knew how nasty a little harmless messing around could be, particularly when a small kid with a limp became the target of a bunch of bullies like Brad, his sidekick and their cronies.

"I said move it. And that goes for the rest of you too. Hit the showers *now*."

"Right." Brad and the rest of his "buddies" made for the showers. As they went, Toby smirked at Ryan.

"Gimp," he said.

CHUCKY AND RYAN WALKED HOME, THE SUBURBAN STREETS darkening under the long shadows of the fall afternoon. As they walked, they tossed a football between them.

Ryan lofted the ball and Chucky caught it neatly. "You got gypped, you know that, man? That was your call. Brad knows it. Coach should know about it—hell, the whole *school* should know about it." He dropped back a few feet and tossed the ball to Ryan. "Maybe on Monday, when we get to school, I'll put it out through my highly secret network of agents that Brad and Coach Turner owe their big win to the secret power behind the throne—Ryan Jeffers."

Ryan caught the ball and shrugged as he did so. "Why bother?" he said, an edge of bitterness in his voice. "What's the difference? You could print it in the paper and no one would believe you. Besides, all you'll do is get Brad pissed off big time and I don't think you want to do that, do you?"

Chucky stopped in the middle of the sidewalk and looked at his friend critically. "What's the difference? That's the point. You. *You* made the difference."

"C'mon . . ."

"No. Really," Chucky insisted, unwilling to let it drop. "If Brad had gone with the coach's play, he would been sacked on the forty—or Toby would have been tackled on the thirty-eight-yard line and the clock would've run out. They win, we lose. End of story. But you gave Brad a play that changed everything, won the game for our side—and he gets all the glory." Chucky, who had had a very small share of glory in his twelve years, shook his head at his friend. "Ryan, doesn't that get you mad? Not even a little bit? If it was me, I'd want to punch something. I'd be bouncing off the walls."

Ryan shrugged again and smiled. "Yeah . . . I suppose so. Maybe a little, I guess."

Before Chucky could speak again, several kids on bikes came around the corner and raced down the sidewalk, forcing Ryan and his friend into the gutter. It was Brad, Toby and a couple of football cronies, along with Tracy—the boys acting as if they owned the world, as usual.

Chucky had suffered enough humiliation for one day. Normally he would have meekly gone along with being shoved off the sidewalk, but not today. Not after what had happened. Before he realized it, he was shouting.

"Hey! Watch it!" he yelled after the cyclists. "Can't you see we're walking here?"

"That's tough!" shouted Toby over his shoulder. There was a loud burst of raucous laughter from the group, as if Toby had unleashed a really devastating witticism.

Chucky, really mad now, didn't care what he said next. "Hey, Brad! Ryan called your winning play! Aren't you even gonna bother to thank him for making you look good. Well, that's just like all you guys—"

Suddenly, Brad skidded his bike to a halt, then came pedaling back toward Ryan and Chucky.

"Nice going, Chuck," Ryan mumbled. "If we're lucky, we'll escape with cuts and bruises."

Because their leader had turned back, *all* the riders had to turn back. They screeched and skidded, rode up on the lawns fronting the sidewalk and came bombing back. In a matter of seconds, Ryan and Chucky found themselves surrounded by football players. Tracy, Ryan noticed to his disappointment, had turned around too. Why did *she* want to witness his humiliation? The girl didn't get right in the middle of the group, though; she stood a few yards away, looking on with interest.

"Did you say something, Chucky?" asked Toby, sneering. "Or was that a fart I heard?" There were the usual guffaws that tend to erupt from a bunch of cocky twelve-year-old jocks when bodily functions and/or private parts are mentioned aloud.

Chucky went red to the tips of his ears, but he had already decided that this was no time to act intimidated, no matter how panicky he might really feel inside. He made an elaborate show of sniffing the air, inhaling deeply, then shaking his head.

"I don't smell anything, Boner Brain." Strangely, although a body part had been mentioned, no one laughed. Toby, Brad and the rest of them just

41

stared at Chucky, amazed that he had found the courage to insult one of the elite of the school.

Chucky decided to harness the element of surprise and pushed on with his defiant words.

"Hey, Ryan called that final play, you know. You heard him. I know you did. The whole offensive line heard him." Chucky turned to Brad. "Ryan told you exactly what to do—and you did it."

Ryan knew that Chucky was coming dangerously close to getting a punch in the teeth and tried to pull him back from making things any worse for either of them. But Tracy smiled when she heard Chucky's fighting words. She sauntered over to her boyfriend, a smirk on her pretty face.

"*Reeeally,* Brad," she said, her eyes flashing. "I thought you said that play was your ingenious idea." Tracy laughed, enjoying Brad's moment of acute discomfort. Ryan's head was reeling. He didn't know what surprised him more—that Chucky had spoken up or that Tracy was more than a pretty face. That she could tease her boyfriend, instead of timorously going along with the general hero worship. It made him like her more—if that was possible.

Brad turned and faced Ryan, his jaw tight and his eyes blazing. For a moment or two it looked like Brad was going to hit him, but at the last moment his expression changed, easing up a little.

"Yeah," said Brad, nodding slightly. "Bootleg left, clear path all the way to the end zone. It was a good call, man. Really good."

Both Ryan and Chucky were taken aback by this unexpected display of good sportsmanship from an unlikely source. It was so surprising that they both half expected the world to come to an end in that very moment.

"Thanks," said Ryan.

But the good sportsmanship could not last long. "Too bad you can't play," said Brad. "You're pretty smart."

Chucky nudged Ryan in the ribs. "Come on, Ry," said Chucky quietly. "Let's get out of here."

The two boys turned and started to walk away. "Wait," Brad called.

Chucky and Ryan stopped and looked back. "Yeah?" said Ryan.

"You wanna hang out with us tonight?" Brad asked casually, as if it was a question he asked Ryan and Chucky every day of the week.

Ryan looked as if someone had dumped a bucket of cold water over him. "Tonight?" He paused a moment, as if consulting a date book in his mind. "Yeah . . . sure . . ." He was trying to keep his voice light and offhand, as if he wasn't completely astonished by Brad's sudden cordiality.

Brad nodded. "Cool. We'll be at the Orono Tunnel at eight." He pointed to Chucky. "You too, up-Chuck."

"Great," said Ryan. "We'll be there."

But there was more—Brad put out his hand and he and Ryan shook. Then he got back on his bike and pedaled away, his entourage following. As they went, Tracy looked back over her shoulder and smiled at Ryan.

"Jeez," said Ryan. "What a weird day."

Chucky just stared at him. "Weird? What's the matter with you? You got a death wish or something? The guy's evil, Ry. He's gotta be planning something. Come on—guys like Brad, Toby, the others, they aren't the kind who say 'Ooops, we made a mistake and these guys are cool after all.' You gotta realize that much. You made him look bad in front of the team, in front of his girlfriend. He's got something planned and I don't want to know what it is."

"What do you mean *I* made him look bad?" Ryan asked, his voice irate. "You were the one who had to open your mouth and rub his nose in it. You're the one who ruined his day. Not me."

Chucky thought about this simple fact for a moment or two. "I see your point," he said.

"So you're not coming tonight?"

"You're really going to go?" Chucky asked.

"Yeah," Ryan said firmly. "I'm going to go. I mean . . . they're not going to *kill* us or any-

44

thing." Then he added after a moment, "Are they? I mean, not even those guys are so stupid to commit premeditated murder. That could even get *those guys* in trouble."

"Yeah, but they wouldn't do any prison time until the football season was over." Then Chucky turned serious. "Did you hear where they want us to meet them? Doesn't that tell you something?"

"The Orono Tunnel? So what?"

"Ever been there?"

Ryan shook his head. "No."

"Know anything about it?"

"A little . . ." He shrugged. "I mean, I've heard kids talking about it. That's all."

"Its part of the county drainage system. It's a tunnel. It's a big, deep, black hole in the ground that's filled with deep, black water. Does this sound to you like the kind of place you might want to hang with anybody? I mean, it does not exactly sound inviting, does it?"

"So," said Ryan. "I take it this means that you're not going to go. Is that it?"

"I didn't say that," said Chucky. Suddenly he broke into a broad, mischievous grin. "After all, you *are* the man. I'll see you there, okay?"

Chucky broke away, making for some houses. Then he started to run. "And it's Rice down the line," Chucky yelled, doing his best sports announcer imitation. "He's open! Rice is open! Pass!"

Ryan reached back and fired the ball, a bullet that went straight into Chucky's outstretched arms.

"Touchdown!" Chucky yelled, capering around in an imaginary end zone, dancing like a fool. "It was an incredible pass from the man simply known as Ry!"

Chucky kept on running, making for his house. Ryan just shook his head and laughed. "Crazy," he said aloud.

3

NOTHING SEEMS LONGER THAN SIXTY SECONDS ON THE timer of a microwave. Kathryn stood in front of the machine, looking at her watch and mentally urging the microwave to work a little faster. The seconds ticked down and finally the oven beeped. She flung open the door and grabbed the dish inside—it was so hot she almost dropped it on the counter.

"Damn it!" she yelled, waving her hands in the air as if trying to blow away the pain. She grabbed a hot pad and held the dish tight, digging a wedge of lasagna out and putting it on a plate.

"Hi, Mom," said Ryan, coming into the kitchen. He noticed that she was still dressed in her work clothes.

"Hey . . . just the man I was looking for," said Kathryn Jeffers. "Dinner is almost served. Fabulous frozen."

"You going out again?" Ryan asked.

Kathryn nodded. "Yeah. Sorry. I've got a showing in about twenty minutes . . . I'm afraid you'll be dining alone. Just one more time, okay, Ry? I'm sorry."

Ryan shrugged, but it was plain to his mother that he was unhappy about eating alone yet again. "That's okay . . ."

"How was the game?" Kathryn asked as she laid a place for one on the kitchen table.

"We won," said Ryan. "Brad got a touchdown on the last play of the game." He opened the refrigerator and pulled out a can of Coke. He popped it and took a swig. "The ending was kind exciting . . ." Then, under his breath, he muttered: "I came up with the play."

Kathryn brightened and beamed at her son. "Really? You did? That's great. I'm really proud of you, Ryan."

Ryan slumped down in a kitchen chair. "Proud? Proud of what? I didn't *score* the touchdown."

Kathryn stopped laying the table and looked at Ryan, maternal compassion in her eyes. "You didn't score the touchdown? So what? You made it possible, you contributed."

"Yeah, right," said Ryan skeptically.

"You were part of the team," Kathryn insisted. "It sounds to me like they couldn't have won without you."

"Yeah . . . well . . ." Ryan knew it was true, but it didn't feel all that comforting.

Kathryn put the plate of microwaved lasagna in front of Ryan. He looked at it and a funny—sort of disgusted—look crossed his face. He looked up at his mother. Kathryn was looking down at the food, an equally unpleasant look on her face.

"Ick," said Kathryn.

"When's Dad getting back?" Ryan asked.

"You saying he's a better cook than me, your old mom?" Kathryn spoke with mock indignation.

"No offense," said Ryan with a little smile.

But they both knew it was true. Kathryn fumbled for her purse and dug a twenty-dollar bill out of her wallet.

"Okay," she said, "I guess you're reprieved. But you need something to eat. How about that Chinese restaurant you like so much? Min's place—my treat."

"*Ming*, Mom, Ming." Ryan sounded frustrated. "We've only been there like a hundred times."

Kathryn heard the strain in her son's voice and

looked at him sadly. Her husband traveled a lot for his work and she seemed to be on the go twenty hours out of every twenty-four—it was easy to forget that a child like Ryan was not on the same schedule.

"I'm sorry," she said softly. "Yeah, Ming . . . I know, I know. Your mom's just losing her mind running in and out of that door all day long. Ryan, I have to ask you to bear with me a little longer, just until the rush is over. Then things will settle down, Dad will come home . . . We'll get ourselves back to being a family again, okay?"

Ryan nodded, but was rigid, showing no affection as his mother kissed him on the forehead.

"I'll see you in a couple of hours."

"Okay," he said nodding a little despondently. Once his mother was gone, he slumped down in his chair, looking and feeling like the loneliest person on the face of the planet. Bravo was watching him, but he had one eye fixed firmly on the steaming plate of microwave lasagna.

"Okay," said Ryan. He put the plate on the floor, snatched the twenty-dollar bill and walked out the back door.

THE MOMENT RYAN OPENED THE KITCHEN DOOR OF THE Golden River Noodle Company, he could see that the usual riot was going on there. He was greeted by the predictable wave of hot steam and the continuing commotion of the kitchen. As he stepped across the threshold, however, he almost ran smack into Lang, who was carrying a tray piled high with dishes.

"Stupid kid!" Lang barked. "What are you doing in here? Go on! Out! *Out!*"

Ming looked over from his station at the stove, saw Lang and heard his angry words. With a wink to the other cooks, he picked up a tomato and rolled it on the floor—right into Lang's path. The older man stepped on the tomato, squashed it under his shoe and then flew into the air, the tray soaring above him. Ming pirouetted, kicked out a leg and caught Lang before he fell to the floor, then he spun and neatly caught the tray and put it down on the counter unharmed.

There was ragged applause from the line of cooks at the stoves. Ming bowed to them and then to Lang.

"Be careful now, Mr. Lang," said Ming. "It's slippery in here. You have to watch your step."

Lang looked a little shook up by what had just happened—it never dawned on him that his near accident was no accident—and seemed a little humbled by the experience. As he picked up his tray, Ming turned to Ryan, smiled and winked broadly.

"Hey, Ming," said Ryan. He put out his hand and the two of them exchanged a private hand-shake—closed fists, knuckle to knuckle, then palm side down. Ryan still didn't look happy and Ming could see that his young friend was a little down.

"What's up with you, Ryan?" Ming asked. "Looks like something's got you singing the blues."

"Nothing," said Ryan.

Ming smiled knowingly. "Yeah, I hate it when nothing bothers me too. A real drag . . ." He pushed Ryan toward the door. "Come on," he said. "I'm on my break. I've got something for you . . ."

"What is it?" Ryan asked, a little curiosity in his voice.

Ming stripped off his apron and, without looking, tossed it toward a hook on the wall. The neck strap of the apron snagged exactly where it was supposed to.

"You'll see," said Ming.

MING LIVED IN A SMALL, CRAMPED BUT NEATLY ARRANGED apartment above the restaurant. There wasn't much room, but everything the cook owned seemed to be placed just so—just like in the kitchen. It was as if Ming didn't need a lot of space to live (or work) as long as every object was in the correct spot. The single window looked down onto the skylight set in the roof of the kitchen; Ryan could see the cooks working busily.

52

The Ryan noticed something. "You don't have a television or anything," he said, amazed. "Not even a radio."

Ming was searching through a cabinet full of old books and musty papers. He tapped his head. "I get better reception up here," he said.

Ryan rolled his eyes as he walked over to a bureau. There was a cocoon on the countertop, preserved in a glass jar. He picked it up and turned it in his hands, examining it curiously.

"Hey, Ming . . . what's this thing?"

Ming stopped searching long enough to look over at Ryan. "I found that a long time ago," he said. "I guess I was about your age."

Ryan leaned down until his face was only an inch from the glass container. The cocoon was grayish and the surface was marked with an irregular pattern of bumps and creases; one end was open, a ragged gash, as if part of the cylinder had been ripped away.

"I was on my way home from school," Ming explained. "I saw it lying on the ground, just sitting there, but it was moving slightly, there was something inside it. Something alive that was trying to get out." Ming bent down and looked at the cocoon, close up like Ryan, as if seeing it for the first time.

"Yeah?" said Ryan. "What happened?"

"Well," Ming continued, "I got down on my

53

hands and knees and I looked at it real close. I could see that there was a moth inside, struggling to get out. But he couldn't do it . . ."

"What did you do?" Ryan asked, his eyes still locked on the shroud-gray cocoon.

"I reached down and I tore the thing open," said Ming. "And out he came, takes off into the air and flies away. I'm watching him sort of flit into the sky but then, all of a sudden—*whomp!*"

"What?" Ryan asked. "What happened?"

"Down he comes, right smack into the ground. He's dead."

Ryan was taken aback. *"Dead?"* This was not the uplifting story Ryan had expected. "What happened to it?"

"I interrupted his journey," Ming said simply. "I was not supposed to be part of his life cycle."

Ryan looked at him questioningly. "I'm not sure I get it," he said. "I don't understand."

"We all have cocoons, Ryan," said Ming. "It's the struggle to free ourselves that makes us whole—that's what gives us the strength to spread our wings and fly."

Ryan smiled cynically and laughed shortly. "Its pretty hard to fly when you have a broken wing." He tapped his leg lightly, the one supported by the metal brace.

Ming shook his head slowly and looked at his young friend with a certain note of sadness in his dark eyes. "You're always so certain of that, aren't you, Ryan?"

Ryan shrugged, not sure what to say. But it was an undeniable fact that one of his legs did not work as well as the other one. To his mind, no amount of mystical Eastern philosophy would change the simple, irrefutable actuality of his disability.

From the cabinet set in the wall, Ming pulled a book, an old book with cracked leather binding, uneven parchment pages and an elaborate Chinese symbol embossed on the cover in faded red lacquer.

Ming smiled mischievously. "Remember I told you about ancient Chinese secret . . . ?"

Ryan looked faintly disappointed. "That's all it is? The big secret is an old book?"

Ming shook his head. "A *manuscript*," Ming corrected. "I was like you once, you know. I never felt I was good enough. I always wanted to be like someone else . . ."

Ryan blushed slightly, disconcerted that his innermost thoughts, secrets that he shared with himself only, were so obvious to others.

Ming held up the manuscript as if it were a holy relic, an object worthy of veneration. "But this . . . this manuscript helped me become the person I wanted to be."

"A cook?" asked Ryan incredulously. He was

well aware that being a cook in a Chinese restaurant was a perfectly honorable profession, but even Ryan, in his self-doubt and self-consciousness, had aspirations and goals set a little higher than that.

"No . . . *myself*." He pointed to the symbol etched into the leather on the cover of the book. "This . . . this is Tao. It means the way to yourself. Being the person *you* want to be." Ming held out the book, as if he were conferring an honor. "Here," he said, "take it."

Ryan took the book, but shook his head as he did so. He was pretty sure where Ming was going with this and he was sure he did not want any part of Ming's plan, no matter how well intentioned it might be.

"I don't need any self-help books, Ming," he said firmly, bitterly. "I've gotten all of those I can handle from my mom." He handed back the manuscript. "No offense, but she doesn't get it either." He glanced at the old clock on the wall. "Look," he said quickly, "I have to go. I just stopped by to say hi."

Ming picked up the backpack that Ryan had hung on a chair and stuffed the manuscript into it. There was an enigmatic smile on his face. "This isn't like the books your mom gave you." He threw the backpack across the room. "Here," he said. "Check it out. It's yours."

Ryan stared at him for a moment, then shouldered his backpack. "Catch you later, Ming."

Ryan opened the door, but just before he left the room, he looked back at Ming. He had become merely a shadow as he leaned back in his chair.

4

RYAN AND CHUCKY STOOD IN THE THICKET OF THE concrete pillars that supported the highway overpass, the ugly, icy glare of the halogen lamps lining the freeway filtering down on them. Behind them was a rusted, dented metal door set in the side of a concrete bunker. A nicked and faded "Danger—No Entrance" sign rocked on its moorings as the wind hit it. Litter and debris swirled in the sudden gusts, and thunder rumbled in the far distance.

Chucky could hardly stand still, hopping from foot to foot as if needing to keep warm, but he was nervous and apprehensive, fidgeting his way through his anxiety.

"Man," he said, "this place makes me itch. It's creepy. Ry, let's get out of here."

"*What?* This is our ticket. We're in, so don't blow it, okay?"

In truth, Ryan wasn't feeling all that confident himself, but he managed to quell his feelings, in hopes that something good would come of this evening. It was worth the risk. If they were accepted by the football team, then they would be hanging with the coolest crowd in the school. That could open certain social doors that were closed and locked to them now.

"Man, I hope you're right . . ." Chucky sounded far from convinced that they were making the right move. "Maybe they won't come," he said, hopefully. "We were here—they weren't. So all bets are off."

Then he saw some small lights in the distance—they were moving toward them and he nudged Ryan in the ribs.

"Looks like they're gonna show up after all," said Ryan.

"Great," said Chucky unhappily.

Within seconds Brad and his cronies pulled up on their bicycles. Ryan was a little surprised to see that Tracy had come along too and it made him feel slightly better. Girls—usually more levelheaded than boys—would not go along with anything dangerous or illegal.

"So, " said Ryan, stepping forward and speaking with a confidence he did not really feel, "what are we gonna do here?"

Brad tossed away his bicycle and pulled a flashlight from his pocket. "We're gonna play a game."

"A game?" asked Chucky nervously. "What kind of game?"

"A real simple game, Up-Chuck," said Brad coldly. "You probably played it when you were a kid . . . It's called Follow the Leader." He stepped over to the steel door and pulled it open. The hinges creaked like something out of a haunted house. The darkness beyond was impenetrable, so dark it looked dense, as if you could put out your hand and touch it.

"Who's the leader?" Ryan asked suspiciously. "You, right?"

Brad shook his head. "Wrong. You are." He pointed to the tunnel entrance with the flashlight. "After you."

Ryan and Chucky exchanged quick looks, then cautiously stepped into the darkness. Brad, Tracy and the rest of the cronies followed.

The tunnel was narrow and damp and it had been cut through solid rock, rough hewn, sweating cold moisture. Ryan and Chucky led the way, illumination from Brad's flashlight coming from behind them, but only able to penetrate a few feet into the murk ahead. There were old railway ties and rails beneath their feet and they had to go slowly to avoid stumbling. Drops of cold water fell from the ceiling like an intermittent rain. From the moment they stepped into the tunnel Ryan and Chucky had felt that they were deep underground, buried in the bowels of the earth, but as they walked they could still hear the rumbling of thunder outside. It did not make them feel any better about their predicament.

"Bad idea, Ry," Chucky whispered. "A very bad idea."

"Just relax, okay?" Ryan hissed back.

But Chucky refused to relax—in fact, he was incapable of it. "I told you, something's up . . . and its going to get worse . . ."

"Chucky . . ."

"They've taken us down here to carve their initials in our chests," Chucky babbled nervously. "Or make hot dogs out of our wieners. *Hot dogs, Ry* . . . With meatballs on the side."

"Chucky, shut up!"

They reached the end of the tunnel. The passage dead ended in a concrete wall.

"Now what?" asked Ryan, turning and squinting into the beam of the flashlight.

The shaft of light dropped from his face and rested on a disk of rusty metal set in the stone floor of the tunnel.

"Now *that*," said Brad. "Come on, Toby." The two boys squatted down and levered up the heavy manhole cover. As the hatch came loose, a waft of dank steam, a vapor smelling of sewage and still, old water, floated up into the air. Ryan's nose wrinkled at the noxious odor and he looked over at Chucky. The terror on his face was obvious. Ryan wondered if he looked as scared as his friend.

Chucky did his best to make his voice sound light. "Me, oh, me, oh my," he managed to croak. "I just remembered . . . I've got a Spanish test tomorrow." He turned, ready to make the journey down the tunnel, by himself and in the dark, rather than go down that manhole. "So, adios, amigos." He gave Brad and the cronies a jaunty little salute and then took a step down the tunnel.

Toby grabbed him. "I don't think so, Up-Chuck."

Brad pointed down into the manhole, grinning slyly. "That way, guys. Down."

They didn't have much of a choice. Ryan took a deep breath and started down the rusty ladder.

At the bottom they found themselves in a wider space, an underground cavern where water from a catchment basin drained into a giant cesspool. Pipes and mechanical dials were built into the walls, but the valves were old and warn and water dripped through the seals. Metal grates blocked off some of the water courses, including a wide spillway. It was empty now, but it was slick with a sheen of wetness. On the far side of the cesspool was a small ledge, a lip of concrete only a few inches wide. Brad let the beam of the flashlight play along the wall above the projection and Chucky and Ryan could see that a number of names and elaborate graffiti had been spray painted there. There was Toby's name and, to Ryan's surprise, Tracy's; it was no surprise that Brad's name was the largest of all of them. The only way to reach the edge jutting out from the wall was by crossing on a set of fiberglass pipes that spanned the water.

Brad put his arm on Ryan's shoulders and leaned into him. "See, to hang with us, you've gotta be initiated. It's really simple . . . Just walk across that pipe and give us an auto-graph . . . Make your mark."

A spray can materialized in Toby's hand. Brad took it and slapped it into Ryan's chest. "There you go, buddy. All yours."

Ryan opened his mouth to say something, but hesitated. Chucky and Tracy looked alarmed, fearful on Ryan's behalf.

"Better get going, Ryan," Brad coaxed.

"W-what's the hurry?" Chucky asked.

Brad pointed to the spillway. "See that? Never know when its going to take a dump. Gotta be quick."

The spillway bisected the length of fiberglass

pipe. If water with any force came down that passageway, it would knock anybody standing on it off and into the roiling pool below.

Tracy stepped forward. "*Brad!*" she said. "You said you wouldn't make him go through with it. You know he can't make it across. Not with . . ." Her voice trailed off, but she glanced down at Ryan's injured leg. Ryan saw the look and he flushed with embarrassment.

"I'll do it," said Ryan.

"Ryan," said Tracy forcefully, "he's just making fun of you. Don't listen to him. Please."

A carefully modulated note of sincerity came into Brad's voice. "Look, we all did it. If you want in, you have to do it too." He shrugged. "It's all up to you, Ryan." He looked over at Tracy. "Look, if it'll make you feel any better, I'll wait for him on the other side."

Brad stepped up and put a foot on the pipe, which sagged slightly under his weight. Even for an athlete like Brad it was apparent that tightrope walking the pipe was not easy, but in a few seconds he was on the far side. He stood on the ledge and took a little bow.

"See, Ryan?" he shouted, his voice echoing off the concrete and cold steel. "Nothing to it."

Ryan felt himself sweating, despite the cold damp of the chamber. He wiped away the perspiration on his upper lip. "Oh, man . . ."

"Come on, Jeffers," Brad shouted, his voice angry now. "You cool or what?"

Chucky grabbed Ryan by the arm and tried to pull him away. "Man, Ryan," he said urgently, "this is just stupid. *Stupid*. Let's make like Tom and Cruise, okay?"

Ryan broke free, pulling his arm away roughly. "Shut up, Chucky! I can do it, okay? *He* did it, didn't he?"

"Yeah, but you're not him," said Chucky flatly. It was a simple statement of fact.

True—though the truth stung. For a moment Ryan stared hard at Chucky, then turned and stepped onto the pipe. Two steps into his crossing it was apparent that Ryan's leg was slowing him down, that he had none of the natural agility of Brad. Each step was a balancing act and a difficult one at that.

A few more steps and he was halfway across the pipe, but his face was dripping with sweat and he could feel his concentration, his small store of self-confidence, draining away. As he took another step, his bad leg snagged and he almost slipped, inches away from toppling into the water beneath. Ryan stopped and gulped.

He stood stock still for almost a minute, unwilling to take another step. He could not bring himself to go forward and he knew he couldn't turn and retreat to the safety of Chucky and the others.

"Move it!" Brad shouted and Ryan flinched, startled by the booming of the kid's voice. "Show me you got what it takes! Make the team, man! You're almost there."

Chucky was beside himself with fear. "Leave him alo—" His words were cut off as Toby clapped a grimy hand across his mouth.

"You in or out, Jeffers? In or out?" Brad shouted.

Ryan's face was a mask of fright and indecision, and he was shaking with dread, but he fought it down, taking a deep breath and summoned up the shred of courage that remained. Under his breath, unheard by the others, he muttered a single word: "in."

He forced himself to take another step . . . And suddenly, that was all it took. He took that one step and his worries lifted, his confidence came flooding back and he knew he was going to make it all the way across. A smile of satisfaction crossed his face and he looked Brad square in the eye, enjoying for a moment his triumph.

But then there was a sound in the spillway, a huge, gushing, gurgling noise. Ryan's face went numb. A split second later a vast stream of water blasted out of the chute and hit Ryan with the force of a fire hose. One moment he was there, teetering on the pipe, the next he was gone, blown from his perch as if he had been shot.

Ryan was aware that he was falling and somewhere, far off, above the roar of the rushing water, he could hear Chucky yelling his name. He could hear Tracy screaming.

Then he hit the water and he was enveloped in silence. Something in Ryan told him to fight, to battle his way back to the surface. He struggled and thrashed, but the water seemed heavy, like syrup, his arms and legs leaden and ineffectual, unequal to the task of fighting the current dragging him down.

Then, without warning, everything went still and Ryan felt himself suffused under a wave of tranquillity and he was floating, but sinking too, fading away into the black calm of the deep pool . . .

5

THERE WAS A BRIGHT, SEARING LIGHT IN HIS BRAIN followed by panic, a sudden sharp fear that pulled him back to consciousness. He was still underwater, but rising, not sinking, battling back toward the surface. His lungs felt as if they were on fire, burning through his chest, but he fought the instinctive craving to breathe in. At the very last moment, when the agony seemed almost unbearable, when it seemed like he couldn't battle any longer, something seemed to grab him and pull him upwards. Ryan broke the surface and gasped deeply, gulping in sweet, fresh air.

He thrashed and floundered in the water, his

head spinning as if he were intoxicated by the sudden influx of oxygen. His feet found the bottom and he stumbled and fell to his hands and knees in the water, then lurched forward, blindly crawling from the water, throwing himself on dry land. He lay there, stunned, shocked, exhausted, his lungs pumping, rising and falling like a pair of bellows.

There was absolute silence—no screams, no roar of rushing water, no shouts and echoes in the dank water tunnels. Slowly, as Ryan returned to full consciousness, he began to realize that he was outside, lying in a pool of dappled daylight, warm, mist-streaked rays from the sun streaming through a canopy of trees high above his head. Ryan forced himself to sit up and look around him.

The drainage pool had become a placid stream, lined on either side by rows of trees connected by dense underbrush. The trees were tall and majestic, so tall they seemed to reach all the way into the sky. The jungly underbrush was like nothing Ryan had seen before, a multicolored tangle of shrubs and bushes. He had no idea where he was—but he had the sense that he was a long, long way from home.

"Chucky? Tracy?" Ryan scrambled to his feet and cupped his hands around his mouth. "Chucky!"

But there was no answer. Ryan felt a cold fear rising inside him . . . Could it be that he was . . .

dead? The awful realization hit him like a hard, stinging slap in the face. Then he felt the sagging weight of his backpack on his shoulders and was reassured faintly. He doubted that you were allowed to bring carry-on luggage into the afterlife . . .

Behind him he heard a noise, the slightest rustle in the dense tangle of vegetation under the trees. Ryan whipped around to catch the slimmest glimpse of—what? An eye. Ears. A thick tail. Then it was gone, and it all happened so fast Ryan couldn't really be sure that it had happened at all. It must have been an animal of some sort . . . Ryan felt a faint tremor of fear. Just about the last thing he needed was to run into some kind of wild beast. Before his fears could get the better of him he said aloud:

"Remember, animals are more frightened of you than you are of them . . ." He paused a moment, then said, "Or is that snakes?"

Suddenly, Ryan felt very tired and his shoulders slumped. He was sick of the quest for adventure and the desire for acceptance. All he wanted to do, right then, was go home. He rubbed his eyes and tried to collect his thoughts. The thing to do, he decided, was to find a road or even a path, something that might lead to someone who would help him.

Ryan squared his shoulders and took a deep breath. He looked up through the awning of interlocked tree branches high above his head, searching for the sun, in an attempt to establish his position . . . Then he realized he didn't know how to do that—it was only something he had seen in movies.

"Oh well," he said and turned to start on his journey. He had traveled about two steps when he stopped, rooted to the spot. His face went ashen and the blood ran cold in his veins.

Facing him across the clearing were ten men, each dressed in black from head to toe. Their uniforms were overlaid with armor, strange jet-black armor, menacing plates with spikes on their breastplates and blades at the shoulders, and the steel was form fitted to their bodies like the carapace of an insect. Their faces were hidden behind sinister dark helmets. Their weapons were primitive. Some of the soldiers carried long spears like medieval halberds; others clutched short stabbing swords. One of them had flashes of gold on his shoulders and on the visor of his helmet and looked as if he was some kind of officer.

"Whoa," whispered Ryan, backing up against the stout tree trunk directly behind him. For what seemed like an hour but in actual fact was only a moment or two, Ryan looked at the soldiers and they looked at him. Then the one with the gold on his uniform gave an order and, faster than Ryan could have imagined, the soldiers were on him, their swords and spears raised. For a split second, Ryan noticed, almost detached—as if he was watching someone else—that these ominous-looking men were about to cut him to pieces with their evil weapons.

Then he screamed and turned to run. But before the swords could fall—before he could travel a single step—there was a flash of movement as something burst from the water of the stream, breaking the surface like a fish jumping. But this was larger, more powerful. It came out of the water and passed between Ryan and the soldiers, throwing the men back.

Of course, neither Ryan nor the soldiers actually *saw* anything beyond a bolt of cobalt blue followed by a strong gust of wind that whipped across the clearing like a dervish, stirring up a cloud of dust and grit and making the leaves shiver in the trees.

The effect of this sudden and mysterious eruption on the soldiers was apparent. Although the tips of their weapons were only inches from Ryan's throat, they froze in place, instinctively aware that whatever *it* was, *it* was a lot more dangerous and powerful than the kid they had at sword point. Ryan could see the eyes of the men through the slits in the helmets. They scanned the forest, looking for the source of the power, and they looked scared.

When the next onslaught came—and it did a

few seconds later—it came from a totally unexpected quarter, this time from above. There was another blinding flash of blue light as something vaulted from the branches. It was like a the cone of a tornado, an intense column of power, a typhoon of swirling wind and debris, that swept through the line of soldiers, throwing them heavily to the ground.

Ryan was flattened against his tree trunk and he did his best to follow the moving figure with his eyes, but as soon as it appeared it was gone again. He could sense the panic rising in the soldiers as they stumbled to their feet, reaching for their weapons.

The wind rose again and the force returned, even stronger than before; it broke from the mist and shadows this time, falling on the soldiers. Ryan could see the heads of the men jerk and snap, their bodies doubling over as invisible blows struck a dozen times or more. The soldiers went down, toppling like a row of tenpins. They tried to defend themselves against whatever *it* was, but the force was too strong.

Ryan had no idea what was going on—but one thing was clear. This . . . this *thing* seemed to be on his side. It had made no move on him, but judging by the condition of the soldiers, it didn't care for them at all. That was all the information Ryan needed right at that moment. He scrambled to his feet and started to run, dashing across the clearing, making for the camouflage and safety of the dense undergrowth. Then something hit him hard in the middle of the back and he tumbled to the ground.

One of the soldiers—it was the officer—had managed to launch a spear and it had hit him square in the back—nailing him in the backpack, the point of the lance not even penetrating the skin. Ryan was sprawled on the ground, winded and scared when the commander raced from his hiding place and grabbed the shaft of the spear, tearing the backpack from Ryan's back.

The man growled as he tried to free the point of his weapon, the better to stab Ryan with it.

"Uh-uh," Ryan screeched, "no way!" He kicked out savagely with his legs and caught the soldier's shin with the toe of his shoe. The man screamed and fell. That was all Ryan needed. He bolted for the woods, running as he had never run before, not noticing—not caring—where he was going. He plunged through the shrubbery and the thickets of small trees, speeding, darting, twisting, rolling left and right, carving his own path through the woods.

Suddenly, Ryan realized what he was doing—*he was running*. And he was running on *both* legs! As he ran, he looked down and saw that his "bad" leg was working perfectly. Ryan shook his head as if to clear it, bewildered by the latest in a series of amazing events. He blazed through the forest, moving faster than he'd ever moved in his life. Branches and leaves slapped against his blue jeans and sweatshirt, but it didn't matter. Ryan was feeling no pain—he wasn't even scared anymore—instead, his spirits were soaring and a great sense of exhilaration washed over him. He was *running*!

Ryan ran as far as he could, as fast as he could, running until he was out of breath. He slowed down reluctantly, his chest heaving, but knowing that he had put enough distance between himself and the soldiers. He was completely stunned by all the weird happenings of the last few hours—the most astonishing of which was the miraculous recovery of his leg.

All he could do was stare at his leg, as if he had never seen it before. It was, however, the same leg. It looked the same, it felt the same. It just *worked* differently. Ryan bent down and felt his leg, caressed it, stretched it, kick out with it like a kickboxer, then jumped up and down on it.

He could not believe it!. "Oh my God!" he shouted, not caring who heard him. "It works! My leg! It really works! I can't believe it!"

Ryan was light-headed with joy and he laughed happily, capering around in the woods. Then he danced on the spot, tried a Moonwalk, gave that up and pretended that he was a quarterback, taking the snap from the center, then dropping back, arm cocked, to fire a bullet-straight pass at an imaginary, but wide open, receiver. Ryan could almost hear the crowd going wild as he connected to score the winning touchdown of this crucial, championship game . . .

But then, like a quarterback who had rolled out of the protection of the pocket, Ryan became aware that someone was—or was it something?— was coming at him on his blind side. There was a noise in the vegetation as a figure blundered out from cover. Ryan did not bother to hang around to find out who the interloper was.

He yelped loud and forgot the imaginary game, quickly putting both good legs to work once again, charging through the woods in a desperate attempt to get away.

But his escape was no more effective than a desperate quarterback scramble—he had only gone three or four yards when he was tackled, hard, from behind. He could feel strong arms encircling his legs and he struggled and kicked, lashing out in a frantic attempt to free himself from the iron grasp. Ryan flailed and squirmed, but he couldn't get free. He opened his mouth and screamed out in terror, certain that this time his life was well and truly at an end. With eyes closed tight he waited for the fatal blow.

"Be quiet!" growled Ryan's attacker.

There was something not too terribly frightening about that voice. Ryan opened his eyes a crack to peek at his attacker. It was not one of the soldiers. No, this culprit was different—far less threatening than any of the armed men Ryan had already encountered. This guy was a man no larger than four feet in height, dressed in clothes all brown and drab green, as if camouflaging himself against his environment.

As soon as Ryan saw him, he stopped screaming, momentarily reassured by the harmless look of the little man.

"Get off me!" Ryan shouted sternly.

"Oh no!" snap the small man. "You're not getting away from me the way you did from those Dragoons, Newcomer."

"Let go!"

"No!"

Ryan had never hit anyone before in his entire life, but he was a little sick of the treatment he had been getting so he did not hesitate to pick up a tree limb that was lying on the ground and unceremoniously swat his little attacker on the head with it.

"Ow!" the little man shrieked. He let go of Ryan's legs to rub his head vigorously. Ryan scrambled to his feet just as the small man did. He looked extremely annoyed at Ryan.

"That hurt!" he said angrily. "Now you're gonna get it." But before he could lay a hand on Ryan, a dagger shot through the air, caught a piece of the little man's clothing and threw him back against the trunk of a stout tree, pinning him neatly. Once he was stuck there, another knife whispered out of nowhere and nailed another scrap of cloth to the tree.

The little man's eyes grew wide and he looked as if he was about to give into overwhelming panic. "Hold the blades!" he shrieked loudly. "Hold the blades!"

Ryan did not know what to expect next—but he would never have guessed who had saved him. A figure was gliding through the woods toward him and Ryan turned to face . . . her. She was a young woman of incredible beauty, with eyes as blue as the ocean and creamy skin that looked as if it was as soft as the finest silk.

She turned those magnificent eyes on Ryan and looked at him closely. "Are you hurt?" she asked. Her voice was soft and musical and Ryan could smell her faint, sweet scent. This vision wore her hair in a profusion of tight ringlets that fell in blond cascades to her slim shoulders. Her slight body was wrapped in a diaphanous gown that covered her from her neck to her sandal-shod feet.

"Yeah. Yeah," said Ryan, finding his voice at long last. "I'm fine, I guess."

This woman was so amazingly beautiful that Ryan sort of forgot the terrible things that had happened to him recently. Suddenly, he felt a *lot* better. He ran his fingers through his hair and hoped that he didn't appear too wet and bedraggled, though he was aware that he was not looking his best. Still, there was nothing he could do about it . . .

The little man was still pinned to the tree, but squirming in an attempt to free himself.

"He's a Newcomer, Elysia!" he screeched. "He came right up out of the river. I saw him do it with my own two eyes. And that means he belongs to me. He's mine!"

Elysia looked at Ryan curiously. His jeans, sweatshirt and running shoes looked extremely exotic to her. "Is that true?" she asked. "Are you really a Newcomer?"

Ryan did his best to reconstruct the events that had led him to this strange predicament.

"Well, I fell in the water . . . I, I slipped . . . and then . . . and then those things . . . they tried to kill me," he babbled.

"Komodo Dragoons," the little man filled in.

"Mudlap!" Elysia said sharply. "Be quiet!" She turned her attentions back to Ryan. "And then what happened?" she asked.

"They tried to kill me," Ryan repeated. "So then I ran . . . I . . ." He looked down at his leg. "I can *run* . . . ," he gasped in amazement.

Elysia plucked at his sleeve. "You must come with me," she said. "Come on."

Ryan tensed and tried to collect his thoughts. "*Wait!* Okay, Ryan . . . Just chill. Chill, okay . . . This is a dream. Just a really intense dream . . ."

He glanced over at the little figure that Elysia had called Mudlap and tried to fit him into the puzzle. "There *is* a Munchkin . . ."

Mudlap didn't know what a Munchkin was but he knew he didn't like the sound of it. "Munchkin!" he said indignantly.

"But there's no yellow brick road . . . I'm not from Kansas . . ." He looked at Elysia. "You're not Dorothy, that's for sure." He rubbed his eyes hard and tried to focus. "And I know . . . I *know* this isn't Oz. Okay, then . . . *Where on earth am I?*" He looked at Elysia questioningly. "Do *you* know?"

But Elysia was looking back down the track. Ryan could see fear in those blue eyes.

"Those were Komodo's men," she said apprehensively. "We're not safe here. Let's go."

"Komodo?" said Ryan. He didn't like the sound of that name at all. And it was apparent that the word made Elysia nervous as well. She looked down the track again.

"We *must* go," she said.

"Where? Go where? Where *am* I?"

"We must go to our Lifespring," said Elysia quickly. "It is within the Radius of Green."

"In the what?" Ryan asked.

"You're in Tao, Newcomer," said Elysia. "Tao."

And before Ryan could answer, she grabbed Ryan's hand and yanked him hard—pulling him *straight up into the air!* Ryan was too astonished to

81

utter a word, but as they shot up into the latticework of branches, he could hear the man Elysia called Mudlap, still pinned to the tree, shouting after them. His voice was high and irate.

"Elysia! *Elysia!* What about me? You can't leave me here! And you can't steal my Newcomer! What about a small reward for my efforts? If it hadn't been for me—"

"Keep the daggers, Mudlap!" Elysia shouted back. "That should be compensation enough."

Mudlap tugged at his clothing, working to free himself. It was obvious that the tiny man was furious, fuming and hopping mad. "Bah!" he muttered under his breath. "Virtue be yours, Elysia. Virtue be yours."

6

A DARK AND GLOOMY HAZE OF PUTRID AIR HUNG OVER THE fortress, the citadel home of Komodo. It was a long, rounded structure of enormous size that stood out against the sullen sky. The fortress could be seen for miles, a dark stain on the horizon, not just because it was huge, but because the surrounding landscape was nothing more than a featureless desert, lifeless, dry and barren.

The rolling hills surrounding the castle had once been thick with green forests, but now were scorched and infertile, with only the occasional scrubby, skeletal tree clinging to life in the desolate landscape. The plains spread before the hills were parched now and dotted with foul-smelling cesspools of dark, oily standing water. Even the sky was painted in muted tones of brown and orange, as if glutted with smoke and pollutants. This was Komodo's domain.

There had been a time when all of Tao had looked like the leafy-green place that Ryan had landed in, a small paradise with beautifully lush vegetation, clear running water and peaceful, peace-loving inhabitants who lived in harmony with nature. Until the coming of Komodo, that is.

Komodo had subverted the natural order of life in Tao. He had turned some of the inhabitants into his soldiers, the fearsome Dragoons, and a great many more into his slaves, who toiled in vast labor camps. The remainder, like Elysia and her cohorts, had fled into the mountain stronghold and become rebels, dedicated to destroying Komodo before he destroyed the entire land.

The worst of Komodo's many crimes was the careless destruction of the ecological balance in Tao. The areas under his control had become barren and polluted badlands.

Except for the high towers and parapets built to survey the surrounding sterile plains and hills, much of Komodo's fortress had been constructed beneath the ground. It was a huge, Gothic armaments factory, a vast underground complex of workshops and dungeons built into the side of a jagged gorge, a hideous confluence of waste, minerals and machines.

Everywhere the earth was polluted and the very atmosphere itself was dark and toxic, the nether regions of the fortress populated by workers, drones who scurried like rats in the gloomy, low-ceilinged galleries, dressed in tangles of filthy rags. Except for Komodo and a few of his top lieutenants, everyone in Komodo's territory moved with a scuttling, hunched over posture, reflecting the subservience that comes with lives lived in a perpetual state of fear.

Large hoses, like tentacles, extended from the rear of the fortress, penetrating the innards of a spring—or what had once been a spring. The Lifesprings were the origin of all life in Tao, pools of water fed from the deepest parts of the earth. The site of each Lifespring was the meeting place of the five essential elements: water, earth, fire, wood and metal—the metal being Zubrium, an ore unique to Tao. The harmonic merging of the five elements, with Zubrium as the catalyst, was necessary to produce the powerful positive energy emitted by the Lifesprings. This interaction also purified the water and produced the spectacular jet of water. All the inhabitants of Tao depended on the Lifesprings as their sole source of pure water, but the spring nearest to Komodo's bastion was dying fast—a fact that did not seem to worry the master.

The Lifespring was clogged with refuse and a huge pile of dead trees, tangled trunks and branches, a mountain of dead wood tended by dozens of slaves who hauled heavy packs from the spring toward the stout gates of the Komodo fortress.

Inside the stronghold itself, word of the encounter between the squad of Dragoons and the Newcomer had spread up the chain of command, until it reached the ears of General Grillo, the highest ranking officer in the Dragoons, a man second in authority only to Komodo himself.

The Dragoon commander clutched Ryan's backpack in his gnarled hands, the tiny bit of booty he hoped would mask the humiliating beating his squad had taken, not to mention the added ignominy of having failed to capture the Newcomer.

Grillo met the commander in front of the giant double doors that opened into Komodo's throne room.

"I understand that you did not follow orders, Commander," said Grillo, regarding the nervous man with his ice-cold eyes. "Your patrol was sent to spy on their Lifespring. You were not supposed to be observed doing it. You knew what you had to do."

The Dragoon commander fidgeted uneasily.

"General Grillo, I knew my orders and I attempted to follow them to the letter. But we were attacked by super—"

Grillo held up a hand, cutting off the Dragoon commander's panicky excuse in mid-word.

"Don't tell me, Commander." He pulled a small vial from the belt of his uniform and sipped from it. He seemed to derive great strength from the colorless liquid. "You'll have to explain it to him yourself. I have to warn you, though, he is *most* displeased." As the color drained from the Dragoon commander's face, General Grillo seized the huge brass handles of the door and pushed, throwing the heavy doors open.

"After you, Commander," said Grillo with a slight smile. "We must not keep our leader waiting."

The march from the doors to the throne was the longest the Dragoon commander had ever undertaken—at least it seemed that way. The room was long and wide, a huge barrel of a space with broad, high arches, like giant ribs, supporting the walls and ceiling. The room appeared to be paneled in a yellowish brown stone, an amber-colored substance that admitted very little light. No matter the time of day or night, it was always twilight in Komodo's throne room.

The Dragoon commander continued his slow, lonely trek to his doom, walking between two ranks of soldiers—men he had commanded in the past—and he knew that not one of them would raise a finger to help him if Komodo decided that he no longer needed his services.

In addition to the soldiers and General Grillo, there were three other people—if one uses the term very loosely—in the room, three fearsome killers whose loyalty to Komodo was absolute. One was Mantose, a short, stocky little villain who always spoke with a hiss like a serpent; another was Dullard, a hyena of a man whose taste for viciousness was matched only by his immense stupidity. Most evil of the lot, though, was Barbarocious, a female dressed in robes that made her look like a black widow spider. As the Commander walked the length of the room, Barbarocious watched him, licking her lips and smiling at him in a particularly creepy way.

The Dragoon commander went as far as he dared and then knelt, his head bowed like a penitent. No sooner had his knees touched the ground than a trapdoor in the ceiling slid open silently and a cocoon-shaped pod was lowered slowly into the room. A man could be seen sitting in the pod. Even in the dim light it was obvious that he was something extraordinary, one of mankind's more unique specimens. His countenance, as it looked down upon the Dragoon Commander, was at once brusquely handsome and poignantly beautiful, the face of a goddess as well as that of a god. His fingers, as they toyed with the pommel of his immense sword, seemed tapered and feminine, and yet, when he gripped the hilt suddenly, a network of firm muscles and tendons rose across the back of his hand. His hair was unusually long and luxuriant, but most memorable of all about this man were his eyes, which burned with an icy intensity so fierce that, were you its object, it could pluck out your very soul.

His evil was seductive—those who had seen Komodo's face had been stunned by his physical beauty. Evil fed into the weak and wounded aspects of people, manipulating vanity and greed, distorting perception and excusing thoughts and acts that the clear light of virtue would render repugnant. General Grillo knew Komodo to be the master of this kind of seduction and to use all his senses to subvert, corrupt and terrify.

His voice, for example, was used to remarkable effect. To his soldiers and drones it seems to be everywhere, coming at them from all angles, like the voice of a vengeful god. But one-on-one, face-to-face, Komodo's voice was deep but soft, caressing, lulling the listener into submission. Even his body movements changed to suit the occasion. Occasionally he was like a machine, his movements sharp, stiff, almost mechanical, while at other times he moved fluidly, with the grace of a dancer. At all times, however, Komodo wielded his charisma with a terrible, calculated, ruthless cunning.

Komodo did not move a muscle as he descended into the room, but he never took his eyes from the kneeling Dragoon commander.

There was not a sound in the room and, with the arrival of Komodo, the hardened soldiers, General Grillo, even the three nasty henchmen, grew uneasy. They looked at Komodo with fear in their eyes—he had the ability to keep everyone guessing, no one ever knowing what he was going to do or say from one moment to the next. One thing was sure: the ill-fated Dragoon commander was doomed.

Komodo regarded the man for a moment, then sneered. "Look at me, Commander."

The commander looked up and into the eyes of his superior. He felt the intensity and force of Komodo's eyes, as if his glare were stabbing into him, searing his brain.

"Failure is in your eyes, Commander," said Komodo, his voice deep and resonant. "It is like an open wound. It infects like a disease. And it spreads like an infection. I smell fear. Fear of what? Death? Are you afraid to die, Commander?"

The soldier licked his dry lips and tried to force out a few words. "Please . . . my lord." With trembling hands he held out the backpack, using it as if to shield him against Komodo's anger.

"Look! I've brought this. It came from a boy. A Newcomer."

All of the other people in the room looked shocked at the mention of the arrival of a Newcomer. Only General Grillo and Komodo himself did not seem surprised by this piece of information.

Komodo nodded and held out his hands. That small gesture seemed to unlock some unlock mysterious power that emanated from deep within him. The backpack flew out of the commander's hands, sailed through the air and landed lightly in the hands of Barbarocious.

Komodo looked calm and at ease. "Rise, Commander," he said. This time his voice was light, without the slightest trace of anger. There was even a hint of forgiveness in his words.

The commander looked at Komodo nervously and then slowly rose from the floor.

"I want to take away your terror," Komodo explained. "There is nothing to fear because nothing dies. Life is but one dream, Commander. One dream that flows into another . . ."

The commander had been so tense he felt as if a wire were cinched tight inside of him. Now, with Lord Komodo's reassuring words, he felt that wire slacken a bit, his shoulders slumping in release. Then Komodo made a casual dismissive gesture with his hand, as if waving good-bye to his mightily relieved soldier.

Suddenly the Dragoon commander dropped out of sight, disappearing into a dark hole that had opened in the floor beneath his feet. His screams echoed up the chute, but ended suddenly, replaced by the ugly sound of his bones being crushed.

Mantose, his hand on the lever that opened the chute, snickered, as if enjoying the huge joke of the Dragoon commander's death.

General Grillo looked slightly nonplussed by this—though he had seen many executions in this room before. Komodo caught the faint look of disgust on his subordinate's face and smiled at him.

"I ask you this, General Grillo," said Komodo archly. "What is the point of power if you don't abuse people from time to time? Don't you think so, General?"

General Grillo nodded and smiled. "Of course, Lord Komodo," he said firmly. The general had no intention of following the Dragoon commander into the chute.

Despite the fear that Komodo inspired in all—Grillo included—there was something inherently fascinating about him. He was highly intelligent but despite that he had chosen the course of evil at a very early age. Since childhood his governing emotions had been desire and greed—satisfying his own desires and thwarting those of others, those were the principal sources of his pleasure and gratification.

As a soldier, Grillo admired Komodo's brilliant grasp of strategy and the determination with which he pursued his goals. His vision was one of absolute domination; he believed that control equaled strength and that resources existed for the purpose of being exploited. Komodo was the consummate martial artist, skilled in the most arcane areas of that art—this, taken with his field of Negative Energy, made him lethal. He emitted a cold, malignant energy that Grillo found almost palpable, literally sucking the Positive Energy out of people and the environment alike.

Barbarocious had turned her attention to the backpack in her talonlike hands and she began ripping it apart, tearing into the nylon like a scavenger on rotting carrion. Dullard and Mantose watched for a moment, then jumped in to help her destroy the pack.

The contents of the bag fell to the black marble floor. There was a Discman compact disc player, a couple of school textbooks, a handful of pencils and pens, an electronic handheld football game—and the manuscript that Ming had given Ryan. The ancient book slid across the slick floor and came to rest near General Grillo.

Mantose looked closely at the Discman, fingering the deep puncture in the black plastic where the Dragoon commander's spear had penetrated. Dullard was chewing on a pen, then he slipped on a pair of Ryan's Ray Ban sunglasses. Barbarocious inspected the Game Boy, then brought it to her mouth and licked it, hoping it was something to eat. Her face creased into an ugly grimace when she realized it was not.

General Grillo picked up the manuscript and turned it in his hands. He recognized the symbol embossed on the cover instantly. And *now* he looked startled.

"My lord," said General Grillo. "Look, my lord, it's the symbol of Tao. The Newcomer brought this. Could it be *the* Manuscript. The one which foretells—"

The manuscript flew out of his hands and into Lord Komodo's. His eyes seemed to light up when he saw the pictogram cut into the leather, and he stared at it for a long moment.

"At last . . . At *last*," he whispered. Turning his back on the other people in the room, Komodo opened the manuscript and turned the pages, slowly at first, then faster and frantically. He looked up, his eyes blazing.

"Find me the Newcomer. Bring him to me," he said, anger burning through his words. "Find him and bring him to me *alive*."

Mantose, Dullard and Barbarocious looked up from their destruction of Ryan's meager belongings. All three smiled evil smiles, but only Mantose replied.

"A pleasure, Lord."

As the three made there way from the room,

Grillo looked over at Komodo with a forlorn look on his face, as if he were a child who had been forgotten by a parent. Komodo did not even glance in his direction, but snapped the manuscript shut, the sound like thunder echoing through the vast space of the room.

7

THE ATMOSPHERE WITHIN THE RADIUS OF GREEN WAS peaceful and serene, but Ryan's mind still whirled. Elysia had led him through the woods to the river. Carefully concealed on the shore was a raft, hidden under the tall trees that lined the bank, low green branches brushing the surface of the water. Ryan helped Elysia push the craft out into the river, then they clambered aboard, each of them taking an oar to guide the vessel downstream.

"Now . . . *who* are you?" he asked. "And *where* am I?" The raft glided on the river, scarcely making a ripple in the cool blue water.

"I am Elysia," the young woman explained patiently. "And you are in Tao."

"Tao?" he said. Far off, way in the back of Ryan's befuddled brain, the faintest bell rang. The word sounded familiar. He wracked his brain trying to place it—but so much had happened in such a short time . . . "Tao," he repeated softly.

Then he sat upright, as if goosed by a jolt of electricity, and looked at Elysia, shocked and stunned. He remembered now—remembered where he had heard the word. Tao was what Ming had been talking about in his room above the restaurant. When had that been? Last night? The day before. Ryan had no idea. But there was no mistaking the word *"Tao?"*

Elysia nodded. "That's right, Tao."

"It's just like Ming said . . ." Ryan looked around him, wide-eyed, as if seeing the place for the first time. "It's just like the manuscript. I thought it was a story, I didn't believe him. But it's real. This is really happening. The manuscript worked! Just the way Ming said it would." He jumped to his feet, the raft rocking under his sudden movement. "This is amazing! This is absolutely incredible!"

Now it was Elysia's turn to look surprised. "Manuscript?" she asked, her voice low and intense. "What manuscript are you talking about? What does it look like?"

Ryan pointed to the handle of the oar he was holding. Carved into the grip was the ten-point symbol of Tao, the same emblem set in the cover of the old manuscript.

"That," he said. "That is Tao. The manuscript has that same thing on the cover."

Elysia shook her head slowly. "Could it be . . . ," she said breathily. "Could it be the Manuscript of Legend?"

Ryan looked at her blankly. "The what?"

"The Manuscript of Legend," she said again. "Master Chung once told us about an ancient book that has special powers. He said that should it ever be returned to Tao it could change everything." Hope was shining bright in her eyes as she spoke. "It must be the same one." She spoke as if she dearly wanted to believe that. "Master Chung will know."

"Who's Master Chung?" Ryan asked.

"He's our leader," said Elysia. "He's a good and wise man . . . A *very* wise man. When he came to Tao, he taught the ways of peace and harmony. Tao flourished under his guidance . . ." Elysia looked down and then away, as if there were something sad behind her words.

"What happened?" Ryan asked. Since Ryan had arrived in Tao, ten Dragoon soldiers had tried to kill him and Mudlap had tried to capture and enslave him. It was just his opinion, but there didn't seem to be all that much peace and harmony in Tao these days.

Elysia shrugged. "It didn't last," she said sorrowfully. "Komodo began mining the Lifesprings for a mineral called Zubrium. That was how things started to go wrong . . ."

"Why?" Ryan asked. "What's Zubrium? What's a Lifespring?" He was also about to ask who Komodo was, but he was not altogether sure he wanted to know.

"The Lifesprings are the center of being, they are where we live," Elysia explained. "They radiate energy to all of Tao. But they must have Zubrium. Without Zubrium, they die out. And when all the Lifesprings die, then life itself is extinguished . . ."

In spite of himself, Ryan had to know more. "And Komodo? Who's he? Where does he fit in?"

"Komodo uses the Zubrium to keep himself young and strong," said Elysia. "That's why he is so desperate to get his hands on it. Now, only one Lifespring remains. He'll use all his power, all of his soldiers to capture it. And after that happens . . ." Elysia shrugged, not wanting to put into words the terrible future that awaited them all.

"Can't anyone stop him?" Ryan asked. "There must be something that you can do."

Elysia shook her head slowly. "No," she said. "No one can stop him. He is too powerful. Not even the Warriors of Virtue can stop him anymore. Maybe once they could have, but not now."

Ryan was really excited now. "Warriors? Like Kung Fu? Wait! What do they look like?"

Elysia was puzzled by the Newcomer's lack of knowledge. "The Warriors are Rooz," she said. Ryan stared at her blankly. "You know," Elysia added, "Warmbloods." As if that would explain everything.

"Rooz?" said Ryan. "Warmbloods?" Those terms did not sound familiar to him and did not begin to describe any Kung Fu masters that Ryan had ever heard of.

"The Warriors of Virtue," Elysia repeated. "They were chosen by Master Chung. Selected and trained by him. Their task was to defend Tao and the Lifesprings."

"And they failed?" Ryan asked. In his personal mythology, Kung Fu masters simply did *not* fail. It defeated the very purpose of Kung Fu training and mastery.

He looked at Elysia questioningly, but before she could explain further, a voice called out from the banks of the river.

"Elysia!"

Ryan and the woman turned and looked to the shore. Standing in the tall grass at the edge of the river was a short, odd-looking man. Most of the shiny dome of his head was free of hair, but, as if to make up for this deficiency, he had grown the fringe around his head as long as possible, long gray hair flowing down well below his shoulders. His short arms were full of bags, making him look like a vagrant on the move.

"Who's that?" Ryan asked.

"That's Mayor Keena," said Elysia, waving. As the raft floated by, Mayor Keena trotted along the bank keeping pace with the small vessel.

"Elysia!" he shouted, panting slightly as he ran. "We were so worried about you! You've been gone for so long! You shouldn't go out on these long trips."

"Sorry, Keena," Elysia called back. "I didn't mean to worry you. I apologize."

"Komodo's men have been spotted inside the Radius of Green!" There was a sharp note of panic in Mayor Keena's voice. "It is terribly dangerous to leave the security of the village."

"Yes," Elysia replied. "I know about Komodo's men. I've seen them myself."

"You saw them!" Mayor Keena shook his head in wonder. "Oh my goodness! Everyone here is in a great panic about it! You must be careful, Elysia!" He stopped and peered across the water, as if seeing Ryan for the first time. "Hey! Who's that? Did you bring in yet another refugee? Where did you find him?"

Elysia shook her head. "No, Mayor Keena, this isn't a refugee. He's a Newcomer!"

Mayor Keena put his hand to his ear, cupping it, as if he were hard of hearing. "What? What did you say?"

Elysia took a deep breath and shouted. "I said *he's a Newcomer*. A Newcomer!"

Even from the distance of the raft, Ryan could see Mayor Keena's eyes open wide. Hysteria seemed to seize him and he began capering around on the riverbank, as if unsure of which way to run. Except for the fact that the man's fear was almost palpable, the effect was quite comic. Ryan had to fight to repress a smile.

"A Newcomer! *A Newcomer!*" the little man screeched. He looked as if he couldn't quite believe his ears. "There hasn't been a Newcomer in Tao since Master Chung and Komodo!"

Mayor Keena shook his head slowly and his shoulders slumped. "That's it! It's over. We are doomed." He stopped just short of a towering waterfall that cascaded down onto the shore and flowed into the river. The spray from the cataract washed over him, but he didn't seem to notice. Mayor Keena looked like the very picture of dejection.

"*He's* the mayor?" said Ryan.

"Well . . . ," said Elysia with a small smile, soft and forgiving. "Mayor Keena has not been the same since Komodo destroyed the other Lifesprings in Tao. It was hard on everyone, but

Keena took it the hardest. He's never really recovered . . ."

Ryan nodded and then looked over his shoulder. The stream led into a dark tunnel, a passageway carved through the trunk of an enormous tree that stood athwart the waterway.

The raft passed through the darkness and a moment later emerged into the sparkling light on the far side. They had reached the village and Ryan's eyes widened, his jaw dropped. The river they were traveling pooled to become a small, crystal-pure lake, the water dotted with luminescent coral. Encircling the lake and rising up the hillside were rows of trees as big as the one they had just traveled through, trees taller and wider than the largest of California redwoods. Roots from the giant trees intertwined, level upon level of them, rising up the bluff, supporting walkways, platforms and sloped terraces. Built along these narrow thoroughfares were the homes and workshops of the villagers, a collection of small, modest buildings. The villagers themselves were everywhere—on the bridges, on the platforms or standing along the shore of the lake. As Ryan and Elysia passed, though, no one seemed to notice them—their attention focused on a moss-covered bridge where an old man, a Chinese man, was addressing the crowd. All were listening intently—and some, like Mayor Keena, showed visible signs of panic.

"Wow!" said Ryan. "I've never seen anything like this. It's . . . it's like a cross between a movie and a fairy tale."

Elysia smiled softly. "This is our home," she said.

As they sailed closer to the bridge, a robust figure on the edge of the crowd, his back to the river, turned and saw them. From the back the man looked like—well, he looked like a man, a little thick set, maybe, but definitely human—but once he had turned around, and Ryan got a good look at him, the boy nearly jumped out of his skin.

"*What the*—" Ryan gaped and his mouth dropped open like the tailgate of a pickup truck. The man was not a man at all. For one thing, he had a horn growing out of his forehead and he had a square gray jaw that looked suspiciously like that of a rhinoceros. But he was standing on his hind legs and dressed in clothing. A smaller version of this creature, his son apparently, stood next to him.

The rhino-man glanced at Elysia, then over at Ryan. Not only did he walk and dress like a man, he *spoke* too, though not in any language that Ryan understood or even recognized.

"Hadoo, no ponna," the strange beast said. There was something in his voice that suggested suspicion or mistrust, though Ryan did pay much attention to it. He was busy still trying to get his mind around the very idea of a walking, talking rhinoceros.

Ryan still stared, his face white as if he had seen a ghost. "Wha . . . ? What's *that*?" he managed to stammer.

Elysia answered the strange creature first. "Apuna a friend, Mosely," she said with a reassuring smile. "Apuna, Mosely."

"Who is that?" Ryan asked again.

"That's Mosely," Elysia explained. "He's a Warmblood. That's his son, Moe next to him."

Moe peered around his father's legs and smiled shyly at Ryan. Ryan found himself smiling back.

"Ah . . . but ruputa, Elysia!" Mosely called out. He pointed farther down the river.

Elysia and Ryan looked and saw the moss-covered bridge, which seemed to be stretched above, not the stream, but the village itself. Standing in the middle of the span, the old Chinese man addressed the crowd as if he were speaking from a pulpit. Most in the gathering were, to Ryan's eye, normal-looking humans. But there were others figures, creatures like Mosely and his son, who resembled animals.

The people and the Warmbloods alike, however, were dressed in similar fashion. They wore loose-fitting clothing—vests and tunics and hooded cloaks—all of it colored with the tones of the Lifespring—deep browns and lush greens, blues and reds, and some had decorated these simple garments with pieces of jewelry, brooches and clasps hand-worked in metal and set with rocks polished like gems.

The crowd was far from placid. As the elderly man spoke to them, Ryan could hear grumbles of consternation and cries of alarm. The man, however, held his hands out in front of him, as if trying to calm them down. Despite the panic, the old man's tone was calm and reassuring.

"Listen to me!" he said, raising his voice to make himself heard. "Please, everyone. *Please*, try to calm yourselves. There is no need for any panic. Please . . ."

The crowd responded to the entreaties, the grumbles and mumbles dying down somewhat in response to the these few reassuring words from the old man.

"Who's that?" Ryan whispered to Elysia. He felt as if he was intruding on a family confab.

"That is Master Chung," Elysia said, her voice lowered also. "He is our leader." The note in her voice of admiration and affection for the elderly man was more than apparent.

"I thought Keena was your—"

"Shh," said Elysia quickly. "I want to hear what Master Chung is saying to them."

"We cannot let our fears defeat us!" Master Chung declared passionately. "The Warriors of Virtue will protect us! As long as they are with us, we cannot be harmed."

"But Master Chung," some one called from the crowd. "Tell us, has Yun returned yet?"

Master Chung was silent for a moment, as if wondering what to say next. The crowd seemed to lean forward a bit, as if by getting a few inches closer they could hear his answer that much sooner. Finally the old man spoke and it looked as if his words caused him pain.

"No," said Master Chung finally. "Yun has not yet returned."

Another roar of panic—the loudest yet—erupted from the villagers. A Warmblood—this one looked to Ryan like a yak—shouted the question that was on everyone's mind.

"Then how can the Warriors of Virtue protect us, if there are only four of them?"

"Who's that?" Ryan asked Elysia.

"That's Willy Beest," Elysia replied. "Oh dear . . . Everyone is so upset. They're scared to death."

The crowd was building toward an uncontrollable hysteria; Ryan could feel it radiating off the throng like heat.

"Komodo's soldiers have already been spotted inside the Green," someone shouted, his voice tight and panicky. "What are we going to do, Master Chung! Tell us!"

Before Master Chung could even think of the right reply, Mayor Keena came racing crazily into the crowd and hoisted himself up on one of the platforms.

"Find Yun!" Mayor Keena yelled. "That is what we should do! Yun must come or Komodo will destroy this Lifespring too. Just as he has destroyed all the others."

All eyes turned to Master Chung, waiting for his response to the mayor's call.

"Yun will come back," said Master Chung, his voice filled with all the conviction he could muster. "I *know* that Yun will return. You must have faith. You must have hope!"

"Master Chung," Elysia shouted suddenly. "We have hope!"

The crowd turned and looked down at Elysia and Ryan as their boat glided closer to the bridge and the crowd surrounding it. A murmur blew threw the assemblage like a breeze.

"A Newcomer has arrived," Elysia announced. She opened her arms wide to include Ryan, gesturing toward him as if his very presence gave the village an assured security.

At the sound of her words, the murmur rose in volume, becoming a loud gasp of disbelief. Suddenly, everyone was talking at once, pointing at Ryan, those in the rear of the crowd vaulting up on the backs of those in front, necks craned for a view of the Newcomer.

Willy Beest shook his woolly head in disgust. "Newcomer?" he bellowed loudly. "That can't be a Newcomer, Elysia! He's far too small to be a Newcomer."

There was another wave of grumbling and muttering. Ryan got the distinct impression that the crowd tended to agree with Willy Beest's assessment of his stature.

Mosely trotted forward from the crowd and stood over him, looking into Ryan's eyes. The rhino-man seemed to be about eleven feet tall and Ryan thought it was like looking up at a statue.

"Tunga wareta," said Mosely. He spoke in a very deep voice that seemed to make the raft vibrate under Ryan's feet. "Booma!"

Ryan stared up at the giant Warmblood, his mouth open but no sound coming out. Mosely glared down at him, impatient—it was plain that he was waiting for some kind of answer to his words.

Then, as if speaking to a foreigner—which, of course Ryan was—Mosely leaned in and spoke *verrrrry* slowly, loud and clear. *"Tunga wareta,"* he repeated. *"Booma!"*

Ryan gulped and licked his lips, which had suddenly gone very dry. "Houston," he whispered more to himself than to anyone else, "we have a problem."

Master Chung came to Ryan's rescue. "Let the Newcomer come forward," he shouted.

Mayor Keena nodded vigorously. "Yes, of

course," he said. "Master Chung will work it out. Calm yourselves!"

Ryan could only stare at the people and the bizarre village and its even more bizarre population. The look on his face registered something between utter disbelief and profound shock.

Elysia put her hand on his shoulder and squeezed, reassuring him. "Come along," she said softly. "Master Chung wants to speak to you. You have to tell him who you are."

"I'm not sure who I am anymore," said Ryan, his head swimming. "This is just too weird . . ."

"Come along," said Elysia. "Master Chung is waiting." Ryan glanced up, but the old man was no longer on the bridge.

The crowd parted as Elysia led Ryan forward. As they made their way toward the bridge, Ryan got a better sense of how the village was actually laid out.

The center of the community was the area around the Lifespring itself. He heard someone refer to it as the Council Round. There was a hut in the Council Round and Elysia nudged him toward it, guiding him toward the door.

"That is Master Chung's hut," she said. "Come along."

The interior of the shack was dimly lit, but Ryan could see Master Chung sitting in a chair waiting for him. Despite the turmoil in the village itself, there seemed to be an air of serenity in the small dwelling, as if Master Chung himself could project a soothing calm.

"This is the Newcomer?" Master Chung said, his eyes narrowing to get a better look at Ryan.

"Yes, Master Chung," Elysia replied. She paused a moment, as if unsure of what to say next. "He says he knows of the Manuscript."

Even the normally serene Master Chung looked very surprised by this piece of information. "Do you?" Master Chung asked, leaning forward. "Do you have the Manuscript, Newcomer?"

Ryan had recovered some of his faculties. His brain was beginning to function again "My name is Ryan Jeffers," he said.

Master Chung ignored this piece of information. "May I see it?" Master Chung asked. "The Manuscript . . . It's very important to us."

Ryan did not answer at once. His mind was churning as he tried to make sense of what had befallen him.

"Please," Master Chung prompted. "If you have the Manuscript, I must see it . . ." His voice was intense and vehement. His eyes seemed to glitter under his bushy eyebrows, as if word of the Manuscript was the most exciting news he had heard in years.

Ryan's reply was no less intense. Ryan had seen and heard much that was mystifying since his arrival in this strange land and there was much he did not understand.

He had heard about Lifesprings and Zubrium and about a man called Komodo. He had been attacked by Dragoon soldiers and saved by a beautiful woman. He had seen animals who walked and talked and even *behaved* like human beings.

But most of all Ryan had heard three words— three words that filled him with an intense excitement, an excitement that must have been as fierce that news of this mythic Manuscript had inspired in Master Chung and Elysia.

Ryan looked the old man square in the eye. "Show me the Warriors of Virtue," he said. *"Please . . ."*

8

MASTER CHUNG STARED AT RYAN FOR A LONG, LONG moment, as if looking through his eyes and into his brain, examining the boy's most personal thoughts, dreams and fears. Then the old man nodded slowly.

"Come with me," said Master Chung.

They left the hut and made their way through the village, across a series of bridges and out of the little settlement. Presently, they came upon a screen of vegetation. Hidden beyond it was a set of wide steps of packed earth, curling up along the steep hillside. Master Chung led the way, and though the path was steep, the old man walked quickly and without exertion. Ryan had to hurry to keep up.

The steps led to the summit of the hill, where Ryan found a large, wide wooden platform, which looked out over a stand of trees, a lush, thickly planted grove of timber and green undergrowth that encircled a clearing. A stone wall stood at one side. Beyond that was a large, still, clear body of water, a calm mountaintop lake, the waters lapping the shore gently.

"I trained these five warriors," said Master Chung, his voice low and soft, but filled with pride nonetheless. "They are the protectors of Tao. Each upholds honor and integrity."

Ryan looked around him, searching the landscape for figures. He had to admit that the scene was pretty and serene, but he did not see a single warrior, never mind five of them.

"Do these warriors fight?" Ryan asked Master Chung. "Do they fight with Kung Fu?"

Master Chung smiled—it was an indulgent smile, a smile that suggested that Ryan Jeffers still had a great deal to learn about the protectors of the sacred Tao.

"They use the forces of nature," said Master Chung, his voice firm and commanding. "The forces of the elements of nature. They are fire, metal, wood, earth and water."

"Oh . . . ," said Ryan. He looked at Master Chung. The old man was looking out over the scene before them—the trees, the underbrush, the lake—as if seeing something that Ryan was not. The silence was so profound, so all encompassing, that it seemed almost tangible. Ryan could not help but wonder what they were waiting for.

Then he felt a breeze, the tiniest whisper of wind, a passage of sweet air grazing his cheek so softly that at first he did not notice it. Then the wind grew in intensity, as if a storm was coming on suddenly, the blast of air blowing through, the branches of the trees waving and stirring.

Then, without warning, a mighty figure appeared in the tangle of tree limbs, vaulting through the branches and leaping vigorously from tree to tree. The figure moved with grace and self-assurance, traveling through the treetops as if walking along a broad boulevard.

At first, Ryan had trouble making out details of this strange creature, so perfectly did he blend into his surroundings.

But as he drew nearer, he could see more. He had searching, intense, bright eyes and a muzzle covered in white fur that formed a pointed goatee under his chin. He was not a man like Master Chung, but a Warmblood. He had long ears like those of a rabbit, but long, powerful legs that ended in fur-covered claws. He looked like some kind of kangaroo.

The creature was clad in a costume made, it

seemed, of wood, bark and timber that had somehow been made supple enough to be woven into cloth. The apparel was predominantly brown in color, but decorated with points of bright green trim. There was a conical hat, also made of wood, on the Warmblood's head, with holes cut in it to accommodate the creature's ears. In his hands he held a long, stout staff, a thick shaft of wood, a deep brown piece of mahogany with a carved grip that resembled tangled roots. On his hips and in bandoliers that crisscrossed his chest were pockets that contained what looked like wooden darts sharpened to stiletto points.

Ryan could only stare as this strange animal drew closer and closer. "Who? Is that . . . ?"

"That is Lai," said Master Chung proudly. "He is one of the Warriors of Virtue."

"Wow!" Ryan breathed. "What's his name again?"

"He is called Lai," Master Chung repeated. "He has the virtue of Order, the integrity of wood. He is meticulous, supremely logical." Master Chung's eyes glittered with merriment, as if enjoying his own private joke. "And I warn you, he is often a bit cranky if you do not do exactly what he tells you to do. He is the rule maker, the maintainer of order." Master Chung chuckled a little bit. "Being so highly disciplined, he feels that it is up to him—indeed his duty—to discipline everyone else."

118

Lai left the treetops, sailing through the air like a bird, landing lightly on his feet at the water's edge. Paying not the slightest bit of attention to Master Chung or to Ryan—in fact Ryan wasn't even sure that Lai had even seen them—the Warrior of Virtue set his feet firmly and kicked at the air. Even from a distance, Ryan could sense the power of the kicks, the double and triple roundhouse blows and the unique swift kick that happened so quickly it seemed as fleeting as a shadow.

As Ryan watched, he realized that he was seeing a display of Kung Fu greater than anything he had witnessed before, greater even than anything Ming had shown or described to him. It was like nothing he had ever seen before and he was entranced by it.

"What . . . what is that?" he asked Master Chung, his eyes wide. "What is he doing? Is there a name for that?"

Lai launched a series of large, fast-flowing hand strikes and kicks. Ryan could see that the Roo kept his body relaxed and fluid as he moved, and was able to deliver the combination of powerful blows though the coordination and focusing of his movements. The staff he carried seemed to be an integral part of the movements, the stout wood coupled with the lithe movements of Lai's body.

"What is that?" Ryan asked again.

"Pek Sil Lum," Master Chung replied. "Maybe you know it as Northern Shaolin."

Ryan had never heard of it under any name. And no sooner had he begun to appreciate the complexities of this new kind of fighting, than another came along. There was a loud *swooshing* sound above his head and he looked up and found himself staring into a bright beam of red sunlight.

Then another figure appeared from above, seeming to fly through the trees like a comet. Another Warmblood Roo materialized, this one dressed in an outfit of orange and red and seeming to dance like a flame. In his hands he carried two long whips that seemed to be made of fire, curling and twisting like serpents, then cracking like shots from a rifle. This creature landed next to Lai on the shore of the lake, the whips in his hands spinning so quickly that they seemed to vanish into the air.

Before Ryan could open his mouth to ask the inevitable question, Master Chung was already there with an answer.

"That is Chi," he said solemnly. "Possessed of the virtue of High Wisdom. He is often very playful, though he is pure intellect. Very imaginative and curious . . ." Master Chung watched the Roo, but did not add that because of Chi's immense intelligence and wisdom the warrior was destined to be a sage. Master Chung suspected that in Chi he had finally found the pupil who would surpass him.

"How does he do that thing with the fire?" Ryan asked, his head still spinning.

"He has the ability to produce fire at will," said Master Chung. "But in fighting he uses his power and quickness to great benefit." He nodded toward the two figures. "As you can see . . ."

"What do you call that?" Ryan asked.

"Choi Lee Fut," said Master Chung.

As Lai and Chi sparred, the ground between them suddenly erupted like a fountain of earth, an explosion of grass and dirt. And from deep in the earth, a female warrior emerged. She wore a simple costume that was green with yellow trim and she looked more slight, smaller and less powerful than the other two Warriors. She carried an intricately carved stone sword, a shaft of heavy granite that she wielded as if it were no heavier than a flower.

"Tsun has the virtue of Loyalty," said Master Chung. "She knows the security of the earth and it makes her kind and nurturing. She has a great love of nature and the land and she has hands that can heal. But her most powerful tool is her presence, as she emanates compassion and healing energy."

"There are girl warriors?" Ryan asked. He looked very puzzled by the sudden appearance of a female Roo.

Master Chung smiled. "I was surprised myself. She was the last Roo I recruited—and, in fact, she came to me one day, daring me to recognize her strengths."

"And?"

"Of course I did," said Master Chung. "Immediately."

But Ryan was still puzzled. "But how does she fight? To be a Warrior you *have* to fight, right?"

"Oh yes," said Master Chung. "Tsun knows all there is to know about being a Warrior. "She has mastered the great skills of Wing Chun, the soft but penetrating fist. And of course, she possesses great skill with that sword that she carries."

As if to illustrate Master Chung's words, she whipped the sword around, a showy flash of swordplay, then joined the other Warriors of Virtue.

As Ryan watched, marveling at all that he had witnessed, another figure joined the scene, the fourth of the Warriors. This one, the largest, the most powerful looking of all, emerged from the stone wall. He was dressed in clothing colored silver and white and looking almost as if it was a suit of armor. He carried a large metal ring and the belts of his clothing were draped with other, smaller circles of iron. Metal plates lined his broad shoulders. This Warrior of Virtue seemed to radiate the power and strength of steel.

"Whoa!" Ryan gasped as he saw him. "Who's that?"

"That is Yee," said Master Chung. "He knows Righteousness and the strength of metal. He sees every choice as right or wrong, with nothing in between. He does not harbor doubt in his mind, and once that mind is made up, he cannot be persuaded to change it. Yee is strong, determined—obstacles do not deter him. He simply moves through them. He does not speak . . ."

Ryan shook his head quickly. "He doesn't speak? You mean, he *can't* speak?"

"No," said Master Chung patiently. "He chooses not to speak. I along with the other warriors respect that choice." There was something in the master's voice that gave Ryan the distinct feeling that he should respect Yee's vow of silence as well.

Yee tossed one of the large metal hoops. It shot forward and then seemed to double back like a boomerang. As it made the return trip, Yee jumped from the wall, somersaulted in the air, landed on the ground and seized the whirling ring in his powerful hand.

Ryan gazed at the four Warriors of Virtue. "I see . . . One is wood, one is fire, one is earth and the other is metal, just like you said . . ."

But then Ryan thought for a moment. "But you said water too." He turned to face Master Chung.

"I thought you said there were five. Where is the fifth?"

Master Chung's face fell and his shoulders slumped. "Yes," he said slowly. "There is another." His voice was filled with disappointment. "The other is Yun, he is their leader. His is the virtue of Benevolence, and the force of water. Perhaps the greatest of all . . ."

"Where is he?" Ryan asked.

Master Chung was silent for a moment, then sighed heavily. "Unfortunately, Yun has lost the will to fight," he said sadly. "When the will is gone . . ." Master Chung shrugged, as if there was nothing more to be said on the subject.

Just then, Chi ignited a flame, sent it to the tip of his daggers and charged at Lai. Lai was instantly on guard, stopping Chi's advance with a swirling block from his stout mahogany staff. As soon as the fight began, the other two Warriors joined in, twisting and turning in the air. Ryan's eyes grew even wider—to see all four in action was even more amazing than seeing the Warriors on display individually.

"They're awesome," he gasped.

As the four Rooz fought, though, the flaming daggers somehow seemed to get away from Chi, flying out of control.

"Perhaps they are," said Master Chung. "But they are not yet ready—" With that the old man launched himself up, flipping into the air, rising higher and faster than any of the others. Deftly, he caught the two blazing daggers, snatching them out of the air, catching them in his robe as if in a fishing net. As he returned earthward, he doused the two fiery sticks in the water of the lake, then darted across the water, ending up next to the four Rooz. He had the slightest look of disapproval on his face, looking at them like the stern teacher he was. The Warriors looked back at their master with respect and resignation. All four of them were breathing heavily.

Even though he was stunned by what he had just witnessed, Ryan couldn't allow himself to be left out. He jumped down from the platform and raced across the clearing.

"Wow!" he said, running up to the group. "That was awesome. Really awesome."

"Who is this, Master?" Tsun asked. "I have never seen him inside the Radius of Green before."

"I will introduce you," said Master Chung, smiling slightly. "This is Lai." Lai stepped forward and bowed his head respectfully.

"And this is Chi . . ." Chi bowed to Ryan as well, but with more energy and animation.

"And Tsun . . ." Tsun dipped her head, bowing from the neck, smiling broadly at Ryan.

"And, of course, Yee . . ."

Yee had a stern, questioning look on his face, but he bowed respectfully—though he never took his eyes of Ryan, as if on guard against the young Newcomer.

Ryan could only do his best to bow clumsily, but he could not help smiling in wonderment. "Hi," he said. "I'm Ryan . . ." Then, feeling as if he should say something else, he added, "How's it going?"

Without thinking—it was a completely natural reflex action—Ryan put out his hand to Yee for a handshake, but the sudden and unfamiliar gesture startled the big Roo, who immediately threw himself into a defensive stance, hands up, feet at the ready to kick, his powerful tail coiled for balance.

"Whoa!" said Ryan, cowering and falling back a step or two. "Sorry. Sorry about that."

Master Chung put his arm around Ryan's shoulder, a protective gesture, as if to show Yee and the other Warriors of Virtue that there was nothing at all to fear from this boy.

"Ryan is a Newcomer," Master Chung told his four warriors, the weight in his words very plain. "A Newcomer who has brought something of great importance."

As he spoke, Elysia came into the clearing, walking quietly, as if unwilling to intrude. She hung back, listening to their talk, but did not attempt to conceal her presence there.

"May we ask what it is, Master Chung?" Lai asked. The wood warrior looked at Ryan ever so skeptically, as if unwilling to believe that this small, rather puny Newcomer could have carried anything of importance into their strange world.

"Ryan has brought a very remarkable thing with him," said Master Chung. "He has brought the Manuscript. The one I have spoken of to you in the past."

It took a moment for the impact of his words to sink in. Chi responded first. "But that is wonderful news! Where is it? Have you seen it yet, Master Chung?"

"No, not yet," Master Chung replied. "Ryan has not yet seen fit to allow me to see it." He sounded slightly disapproving, as if Ryan was being needlessly difficult and proprietary about the precious Manuscript. "He asked to see you before he would deign to show it to me."

"I didn't say that!" Ryan yelped. "You can see the Manuscript any time you want! You can *have* it, Master Chung."

Master Chung smiled. "That is very kind of you, Ryan. And most generous too."

"The problem is, I don't have it!" Ryan felt miserable and scared to say it, but he had to tell the truth.

A look of complete disbelief registered on Master Chung's old, creased face. The Warriors looked puzzled. And it was obvious that Elysia was startled at his words as well.

"What do you mean, Ryan?" asked Master

Chung. "I thought you—" He looked over at Elysia. "Elysia, didn't you say that—"

"I don't have it," Ryan repeated. "I figured that one of you guys must have it."

"One of *us*?" asked Tsun in astonishment. "How could one of us have the Manuscript? We didn't know until this moment that it had entered our world. We did not know about you, a Newcomer."

"Sure you did," Ryan insisted. "Back when you saved me from Komodo's soldiers. Remember? *It was in my backpack!*" Ryan looked from face to face. He had no idea what was going on here, but he was sure of one thing. Even though he had not managed to get a good look at his rescuer, based on what he had seen he figured that his defender had to have been one of the Warriors of Virtue.

"This guy—I didn't really see him, but he was awesome, like you guys. He could move, he could fight. He was . . . awesome."

"The Newcomer uses that word quite a bit," Tsun observed coolly. She was not smiling.

But then the Rooz exchanged questioning glances and it was plain as day that none of the Warriors had the slightest idea what he was talking about—none of them had ever seen him before.

As Master Chung lay back, lost deep in thought, Yee stood up and looked down at Ryan, his eyes

128

burning and questioning, glaring at him. Ryan did his best to look back, to try and convince this huge, powerful, silent creature of the truth of his words. But Yee's harsh, intimidating gazed remained frozen.

It was Chi, the smartest and most analytical of the four Warriors, who solved the puzzle first. "It must have been Yun," he said. "It must have been Yun who saved him."

The other Warriors looked at him, puzzled by his words. Even Master Chung looked surprised.

Chi sighed heavily, as if annoyed at having to explain what he considered a very simple thought. "It's really quite uncomplicated. If the Newcomer was saved at the river—and it was not one of us—then he must have been saved by Yun. It's a simple process of elimination. It could only have been him and him alone. Do you see?"

But no one seemed convinced by the clarity of his logic. Lai jumped to his feet.

"Forget Yun!" he snapped angrily.

"But, Lai," said Tsun, always the mediator. "If there is truth to this . . . if Yun can help—"

Lai cut her off and seemed to get even more angry. "Yun does not care! You know that! He does not care about our cause anymore. We all know that he will not help us!"

Only Master Chung did not seem to share in the anger and doubt that suddenly pervaded the little throng. "In this struggle," he said, his voice calm and low, "*all* five of you must work *to-gether*."

"Five of us?" Tsun asked. "Yun has gone. We all know that. Even if we don't accept it, we know what has happened to him."

"No," Master Chung replied calmly. "It is simple. We must go and find Yun."

Tsun, Chi and Lai looked at one another in wonderment. Only Yee was unmoved. He continued to stare hard at Ryan, his steely, fixed gaze steady and unrelenting.

9

AFTER MASTER CHUNG HAD LED THE FOUR WARRIORS OF Virtue away, Ryan sat on the platform overlooking the Lifespring, deep in thought. He felt lost and scared, unsure of what to do next—not sure there *was* anything he could do to help himself. The other world, the real world, *his* world seemed as if it was a universe away, and for all he knew it was.

He had never felt so completely alone. He had no idea which way to turn, he did not know who to turn to.

He was grateful and reassured when Elysia

appeared out of the gloom and sat down next to him.

"What are you thinking about?" she asked softly.

Ryan smiled wanly. "Oh . . . home. I was thinking about my mom and dad. I was wondering if they were worried about me. I don't know . . . but it must have been a long time since I left." He shrugged and laughed quietly. "I'm not really sure . . ."

"What are your parents like?" Elysia asked. It seemed to be a subject of profound interest to her.

Ryan shrugged again. "I don't know . . . They're parents. They're pretty cool, I guess."

"I wish I had known my mother and my father," said Elysia sadly. Her pretty features were suddenly suffused in sorrow. "Sometimes I think about them, trying to remember . . . something, *anything*."

Ryan stopped feeling sorry for himself and found himself feeling sorry for Elysia instead. "You didn't have a mom and dad?" he said, trying to imagine what that would be like.

"They died," Elysia replied. "They died just after my brother and I were born. Since that time Master Chung has watched over us. He was always good to us, very good . . . but I wish I had known them."

"Where's your brother?" Ryan asked. As soon as he spoke the words, he wished there was some way of getting them back. He could see that Elysia was hurt, that his question had pierced her like a dart.

She hesitated for just a moment or two, but her voice was heavy with emotion when she replied. Her eyes glittered with tears. "He was killed," she said curtly.

It was plain that she did not wish to talk about her brother any more. Ryan let it drop and there was a long moment of silence between them. Elysia broke the silence. Her sadness seemed to have passed a little bit and there was a smile playing about her lips.

"You must have been a great leader in your world," she said. "Only a great leader would be entrusted with something as important, something as sacred as the Manuscript of Legend."

Ryan did not laugh, he did not even smile. He thought about her question. He thought about the foolishness that had brought him to this place, his slavish desire to be accepted, even to the point of accepting a senseless, dangerous dare from Brad.

"Great leader?" he said finally. "No, I wasn't a great leader. Just a bad follower. But I'd sure like to show them now. I'd give anything to have a chance like that."

"Show them what?" Elysia asked.

Suddenly, Ryan jumped to his feet and raced down one of the pathways leading away from the platform. "I'd like to show them that I can run!" he shouted as he ran. He felt the exhilaration of being well and whole. "That I can play football! Do normal stuff, just like everyone else."

Elysia got to her feet too and ran after him, laughing as she chased him, pleased with his sudden playfulness. The sorrow that both of them had felt just moments before had disappeared.

Ryan stopped and looked at her. Elysia was even more pretty when she was laughing.

"What? What are you laughing at?"

"Oh, nothing," she said, as she caught up to him on the path. "I'm just happy. I think I've just found a friend."

Ryan smiled broadly. "So have I."

Elysia gave him an impromptu hug. It only lasted a moment or two, but Ryan was nonplussed—and he liked it. He could smell the perfume on her smooth white skin and the brush of the soft blond curls of her hair against his cheek. The effect was almost intoxicating and for a moment he felt light-headed and dizzy.

"Come on," Elysia said, breaking away from the clinch. "I want to show you something."

She started down the path, running quickly. Ryan raced after her, catching up and running alongside her.

"Where are we going?" he asked.

Elysia just smiled and took his hand, pulling him along. "You'll see. Come on!"

Ryan allowed himself to be led, sure that as long as he was with Elysia he would always be safe.

10

ELYSIA GUIDED RYAN THROUGH A LABYRINTHINE SYSTEM OF paths running along the hillside—they were far beyond the Lifespring now—until they reached a series of ruins. The walls of the ancient village were crumbling; the outlines of the tumbledown buildings still stood but it was apparent that they were fast deteriorating, becoming dust. It was an eerie place, imprisoned by dark shadows, which were split here and there by sharp beams of light that cut through the canopy of tall trees surrounding the place. Carved in the rock in the center of the old village was a face, a giant Roo face, the cold stone eyes looking down on them.

Ryan was overwhelmed and slightly intimidated by the place—by its age, its surreal silence.

"What is this place?" he asked, his voice hushed and reverent, as if Elysia had brought him to a consecrated and hallowed space. He looked out over the sea of ruins and could tell that this place had been built by a more sophisticated culture than the one that lived around the Lifespring in these troubled days.

"All this was built to honor the Rooz," Elysia explained. "During the Old Order they were revered by everyone. They were the nobility, back in the old days . . . Tsun, she's a descendant of the old families. If the Rooz had possessed an aristocracy, she would have been part of it. Ever since the Fall, her family was unhappy about her becoming a warrior. They still remembered the old days, when female Rooz did not do that sort of thing."

"But Master Chung changed their minds?" Ryan asked. "He said that he had accepted her."

"And now her family does as well," said Elysia. "They have to. She is very important to the Warriors of Virtue."

"And the others?" Ryan asked. "Like Yee, for instance. He looks so strong and powerful . . ." Ryan stopped and looked at a statue of a smaller Roo. The stoic stone face from the past stared back. "Master Chung said Yee never talks. How come?"

"He was brought up in the wild," said Elysia, as if slightly reluctant to talk about that Warrior. "He never learned to speak, and yet his understanding of Tao was such that Master Chung saw no need to teach him.

Ryan found himself filled with curiosity about the Warriors of Virtue. They were not as Ming had said they were—they were more than just great fearless heroes; they had weaknesses and foibles, just like everyone else, but they strove mightily to overcome them, fighting their weaknesses as bravely and as ferociously as they would their enemies.

At least, four of them did—the one named Yun seemed to have given up, given in. But he was the one who had so bravely defended Ryan against vastly superior numbers. That simply had not been the action of a warrior who had surrendered to anything.

"Well, then tell me why Yun left," Ryan asked.

"He killed someone," Elysia said solemnly. "He killed someone during a battle."

Now this *really* did not make sense. As far as Ryan knew, the whole point of having battles was to inflict injuries on your enemies. "So? It was a battle. What's the big deal?"

Without warning, Elysia grabbed him by the shirt, shaking him roughly. "It was a *life*! Yun took a life, Ryan."

Ryan was completely taken aback by this.

"Sorry . . . I didn't mean it that way. I'm sorry."

Elysia sighed heavily. "It's just that . . . the Warriors of Virtue have made it their creed—never to kill. But Yun—" She stopped abruptly, as if she wanted to say more but knew she shouldn't. "Someday you'll understand, Ryan. It will all make sense to you someday . . ."

"Understand what?" Ryan could feel the frustration rising inside of him. "What do you mean?"

Ryan could see that Elysia wanted to tell him, that she ached to explain it all to him, but that she knew she should hold her tongue. Finally, she just shook her head sadly and looked at him.

"You remind me of my brother," she said. "He always had so many questions to ask. He never stopped asking questions."

Ryan opened his mouth to ask another one, but he never got the chance. Before he could speak another word, Barbarocious dropped like a spider from an overhanging tree branch above them, sending Ryan and Elysia flying, tumbling to the ground.

Elysia screamed and Barbarocious snarled at her, snatching Ryan up in her long, thin arms. Then she started running through the ruins, carrying Ryan off with her.

"Help!" Ryan shouted. He wriggled in Barbarocious's arms, but the evil woman had him gripped tight, as if her arms were as strong as cables made from woven steel.

140

"Ryan!" Elysia screamed. *"Ryan!"*

Elysia stumbled after the kidnappers, then fell to the ground, weeping. If Komodo had Ryan, then was there truly no hope for Tao? Suddenly a voice came to her, as if carried on an invisible wind. At first she couldn't quite make out the words, but as the voice jeered on, she realized it was calling her name. "Elysia . . . Elysia . . . Come to me, Elysia." The voice stopped as an eerie laughter filled the forest. Elysia couldn't listen to any more; scrambling to her feet, she ran blindly, choking on her fear, in the direction of the village.

As soon as Barbarocious and Ryan had cleared the village and were in the forest again, they were joined by the two other lieutenants of Komodo, Mantose and Dullard, who seemed to have materialized from nowhere.

"Good work, Barbarocious," Mantose hissed as he played with the evil-looking curved-bladed sickle in his hands. "Now, let's get the Newcomer out of here."

The three of them ran through the trees, crashing through the dense underbrush. But they were not alone. In the overhanging branches of the tall trees there was a flash of blue as a figure ran through those limbs, running from tree to tree, keeping up easily with the people on the ground. Then, with a flash this creature leaped from his arboreal thoroughfare and landed on the ground in front of Mantose, Dullard and Barbarocious.

He moved so fast it was hard to see him, but the three disciples of Komodo certainly knew he was there. One moment they were running along, the next they were sprawling on the ground, the powerful Roo tail having swept like a scythe, cutting their legs out from under them.

Ryan lay where he had fallen, dazed by the sudden plunge and the fear that had seized him. Mantose, Dullard and Barbarocious, however, scrambled to their feet to face their attacker.

He was a Roo and was dressed in clothing made from translucent blue cloth. On his head was a hat like Lai's, but this one was a deep blue, the blue of clean, cold water. Ryan knew in an instant who he was. This was Yun, the fifth Warrior of Virtue.

"So, I see Yun's back to play," said Mantose, his voice taunting and mocking. "Where is your sword? And by the way, *killed* anyone today?"

Yun's face tightened and Ryan could see the anger in his eyes. Barbarocious and Dullard attacked first, sweeping forward with a barrage of kicks and punches. But Yun knocked them back with some lightning-fast jabs and kicks that were just blurs to Ryan's eyes. He did not even see the one that caught both of the attackers, throwing them back as if they had been hit by an invisible tidal wave.

Then Yun threw himself into the air, shooting straight up like a bottle rocket—then turned a somersault, spiraling over Mantose to land in front of Ryan, putting himself between the boy and danger.

Mantose did not appear to be afraid. The sickle sliced the air in front of him, fast, murderous arcs slashing back and forth, a killing field for anything in its path.

But Yun was faster than even that. Between the end of one slash and the beginning of another he stepped into the vicious semicircle and grabbed Mantose by the wrist.

Yun then threw his weight behind that hand and deftly turned the sickle around, the sharp, curved blade touching Mantose's own throat, just nicking the skin, causing a thin trickle of blood. Yun had Mantose's own weapon, held by Mantose's own hand, at his own throat; for a moment it looked as if Yun would force the evil killer to slice his own jugular. There was real fear in Mantose's eyes—the fear that his depraved life was at an end.

Then Yun squeezed hard on the wrist, a bolt of pain shot up Mantose's arm and he dropped the sickle. Still holding Mantose's arm, Yun spun him and flipped him neatly into Dullard and Barbarocious, the three of them hitting the ground hard.

Mantose touched the cut on his neck and glowered at Yun with real hatred in his eyes.

"Too good for your own good, Roo!" he snarled.

Yun did not answer, but stood in front of Ryan, his arms crossed on his chest, as if daring the three to come back for more. It was a challenge none of them was interested in accepting.

Mantose pointed a bony finger at him. "One day, Yun," he hissed hoarsely. "One day . . ."

Mantose, Dullard and Barbarocious knew they were beaten. Quickly they took to their heels and flew away through the forest, leaving Yun alone with Ryan.

The boy and the Roo looked at each other for a moment, Yun towering over Ryan, staring down curiously, taking in every detail of what he took to be Ryan's extremely strange get-up.

It was Ryan who broke the silence. "You're Yun, aren't you?" he said. "Right?"

Yun's ears drooped a little. He nodded, but he did seem to Ryan to be a bit sheepish about himself.

Ryan did his best to make the Roo feel better. "I'm Ryan," he said. "I'm the Newcomer. Remember? I'm the one you saved."

Yun bowed his head and then turned away, as if to leave. Quickly, Ryan stepped around him, making sure to remain facing him.

"Hey? Where are you going?"

Yun did not answer, nor would he look Ryan in the face. He kept his eyes downcast.

"Everyone is looking for you, you know," said Ryan, feeling that he had to keep the conversation going. "The Manuscript was in my backpack." Ryan definitely expected to get a rise out of him with that piece of information. *Everyone* in this strange place seemed to be interested in the Manuscript. Except for Yun.

Ryan figured he had done it wrong. "*The* Manuscript," he insisted. "You know the *Manuscript of Legend*! I have to get hold of it and bring it back to Master Chung and the others."

Now Yun was interested. He looked even closer at Ryan. "You have the Manuscript of Legend?" he asked.

Now it was Ryan's turn to do a double take. "What do you mean? You mean you don't have it?" He thought for a moment, then slapped his forehead. "Uh-oh. If you don't have it . . . that means Komodo has it. They are going to kill me."

Yun cocked his head, surprised by Ryan's use of the word "kill."

"Look," said Ryan quickly, "You're going to have to help me try and get it back. Master Chung, Elysia . . . the Rooz—they're all going to blame me for losing it. Please, you have to help me."

Yun shook his head slowly. "I'm afraid you just don't understand, Newcomer." With that, Yun

145

turned and leaped off into the trees, vanishing in the dense underbrush, leaving Ryan alone.

"Hey!" Ryan shouted after the Roo. He was angry now—and a little worried. Without the Manuscript of Legend he was sunk—stuck in this weird and terrifying new world. "Hey, Yun! I was told you're supposed to be some great protector."

Yun could hear the boy's irate words and suddenly he stopped still, listening in the bushes.

"Honor! Integrity!" Ryan shouted. "Remember those things? You can't run away forever, you know!" Ryan stared into the forest, waiting for his words to take hold. But there was no response. Ryan shook his head slowly, sadly, then started to walk back toward the village.

"It's no wonder they gave up on you," he muttered under his breath. "Wimp."

Suddenly *swoosh!* Yun catapulted himself out of the tangle of vegetation, leaping and somersaulting—he turned three times in the air—and landed in front of Ryan, blocking his path. He stared at the boy for a moment, then nodded and smiled.

Ryan grinned happily. "I guess we have a deal . . ."

Yun lifted him and put him on his back and together they thundered off through the trees.

THE ROOZ LAIR WAS ON THE SHORES OF THE LIFESPRING, A meadow behind it. From the Rooz platform you could see the Zubrium pods in the water, their long, bulbous stems rising into the air. There was a steep waterfall feeding into the lake, a glinting torrent of white water.

Yee and Chi sat on the platform, Yee polishing the metal rings against his fur, burnishing the steel shaft until it shone and glinted in the sun. Tsun was close at hand.

Chi sensed it first. He lifted his nose into the air and sniffed, straining to catching a scent on the edge of a breeze. Tsun felt it too. She sniffed, then her ears perked up. Then Yee noticed.

Chi looked into the distance, then his eyes widened, as if he could not quite believe what he was seeing. "It's irrational," he muttered.

It was Yun—Ryan clinging to his back— bounding toward them. It took only a few giant leaps to bring them to the platform. As soon as they landed, Ryan toppled from Yun's back, his eyes spinning. Tsun looked at Yun, then flashed a broad smile at Ryan. She knew what had happened—Yun had not come back to them on his own.

"Thank you, Newcomer," she said.

Ryan just shrugged it off. "You're welcome. Nothing to it."

Tsun turned her attention to Yun. "I always knew you'd come back," she said. "I never doubted it."

There was another *swoosh* and Chi, Lai and Yee

swept up on top the platform, the three of them staring at the prodigal for a moment. No one spoke, then, finally, Chi stepped forward and grasped Yun's arm.

"There was always wisdom in your heart, Yun," Chi said. "Welcome home."

Yee stepped forward and pounded his right fist into left fist twice, then pounded that fist against his heart. It was his sign—a symbol of welcome, of friendship and of solidarity. Yun nodded and grinned, pleased that he had been welcomed home at last.

Lai, however, showed no emotion. He stared at Yun with a very stern look on his face.

"You should not have left," Lai said gruffly. "Order has been disrupted because of it."

Yun nodded. He was well aware that he had not been in his place and that that had upset the natural harmony of the Lifespring. There had to be five Warriors of Virtue or none at all.

"I was wrong, Lai," Yun confessed and looking a little shamefaced. "The Newcomer helped me to realize that."

For a moment, it looked as if Lai was not going to give in and forgive the wayward Yun. Tsun saw what was going on and slapped him from behind with her own tail, nudging him toward reconciliation.

That little poke was all it took. Lai's ears flattened on his head and he sighed heavily.

"It's good you have returned," he said. He clapped Yun on his shoulder. "Very good."

"Yun," Ryan said urgently. "Tell them. Tell them what happened to the Manuscript."

Yun shrugged. "Unfortunately . . . Komodo has it."

"Oh no," Tsun gasped, her face falling.

Chi, Lai and Yee looked very grave, the concern very apparent on their faces.

"With that Manuscript . . . ," said Chi, his voice hollow. "With the knowledge, nothing will stop Komodo now. All the knowledge of the Manuscript of Legend is in his hands."

"There is still hope."

They looked around to see who had spoken. It was Master Chung, who seemed to have appeared from nowhere.

Master Chung gestured toward Ryan, as if including him in the circle. "The Newcomer brought the Manuscript. He is the *only* one with the eyes to see what has been written."

All eyes suddenly fell on Ryan, the five Rooz regarding him with a new level of respect. Master Chung and Yun shared a smile. Then Yun stepped forward and knelt at Master Chung's feet.

"Master," said Yun solemnly. "On my life I will get the Manuscript of Legend back from Komodo."

Master Chung nodded in acknowledgment, smiling down at the Roo. He knew that he would do everything in his power to fulfill this earnest vow.

Beneath the platform, Willy Beest happened along one of the walkways. When he saw the little gathering, he stopped and stared for a moment. Then he raised a hand to point.

"Yun is back!" Willy Beest shouted, his voice echoing down the pathways. "Yun is back!"

As his voice carried, villagers began to emerge from here and there, coming down the paths to the Council Round, amazed at what they saw. They thought that Yun was gone—gone forever. The collective spirit of the village lifted—gone was the doubt and panic, the fear and alarm. The five Warriors of Virtue had been reunited. Yun had returned, just as Master Chung had said he would. The people and the Warmbloods alike broke into spontaneous cheering and clapping, saluting the heroes who would save them from Komodo and his evil minions.

The Rooz and Master Chung knew, though, where the true credit lay. If Ryan had not come into the lives of the Rooz and of the village, then there would have been no chance to reunite.

The five of them bent and lifted him, placing him on Master Chung's shoulders. Ryan beamed. For once, the moment of glory belonged to him and to him alone.

11

KOMODO WAS A VERY UNHAPPY TYRANT. DESPITE ALL THE comforts he could lavish on himself, he was still not content and he blamed the people around him. He lolled on his enormous bed, a rectangle of soft silk and cushions suspended from the high ceiling of his vast bedroom, attended by no less than six beautiful women, the bed being rocked gently by Komodo's body slave, a Warmblood, a chimplike creature named Chila. Yet for all this luxury, Komodo could not rest and relax.

Mantose, Dullard and Barbarocious had returned from their expedition bruised and beaten and looking decidedly shamefaced—not to mention terrified. The three of them had debated the merits of *not* telling their overlord about their encounter with Yun—they could not hide their failure to apprehend Ryan—but had decided that honesty was the best policy. Komodo was furious of course—they expected nothing less than that—but he was known to fly into towering rages when people lied to him or tried to keep unpleasant facts to themselves. It was better to take the tongue lashing and live, than to risk having their deception found out and facing certain death.

The three lieutenants stood at attention while Komodo raged at them, calling them every name he could think of, and when he had done shouting at them, he merely stared sullenly at them, as if they might melt under the heat of his furious glare. Dullard, Mantose and Barbarocious stood absolutely still, not daring to move a muscle. There was no telling how long they might have to stand there before being dismissed.

It was with some relief that they saw General Grillo enter the bedchamber, all three hoping that perhaps he would do something to deflect the anger presently directed at them.

Grillo marched to the bedside and bowed low, trying as hard as he could to be the perfect courtier.

"My lord," Grillo intoned. "We have mined all the Zubrium at this Lifespring. The army is ready to attack."

"Good," said Komodo. He did not smile, nor had he take his eyes off of his hapless lieutenants. He sensed the hesitancy in Grillo's voice, though, so now he shifted his gaze. "But?"

"But now Yun is back, my lord," said Grillo uncertainly. "What should we do?"

"You have heard that Yun is back?" said Komodo. There was a dark scowl on his face.

"Yes, my lord. And I thought—"

"Do not think thoughts!" Komodo yelled, his voice ringing up to the rafters of the room. "You do not think! Do you understand me, Grillo? Your thoughts are of no interest."

General Grillo gulped mightily. "Yes, my lord. I understand perfectly, my lord."

"Yun is of no consequence," said Komodo, waving his hand, as if dismissing the Warriors of Virtue. "When it is time, the Rooz will die. All of them. Even reunited they cannot defeat me. Is that not why they seek the Manuscript of Legend? They need that Manuscript so they can find a way to destroy me. Yes, of course."

"My lord—" Grillo began.

"I said, do not think thoughts!" Komodo snarled again. "Listen to me . . . Beyond these walls, out there, is great anxiety. And I know that where

153

there is anxiety there is opportunity. I intend to exploit that. Do you understand me, Grillo?"

"Yes, my lord." The general spoke a little above a whisper.

Mantose and Dullard spoke in unison, going along with their boss in the hope that they would get themselves off the hook. "They're panicking! They're panicking!"

Komodo stared at them so hard it felt as if his eyes were burning into them. "*Do not think thoughts!*" he shrieked. "If they panic, they will make mistakes. We must let them make their own mistakes."

Grillo understood what Komodo wanted, but he saw no point in risking his neck and his army for no good reason. He summoned as much courage as he could muster and spoke again.

"Forgive me, my lord . . . but if the Manuscript can be used against us, why not just destroy it? It is in your possession. It is yours to do with as you please." Grillo shrugged. It seemed to make such good sense.

"*It* cannot be destroyed," said Komodo. "*You* can be destroyed. Your legions can be destroyed. Everything else can be destroyed. But *it* cannot be destroyed. Understand?"

"Yes, my lord."

"Good." Komodo waved at the women on his bed, at the lieutenants and even Chilla. "You may leave us."

General Grillo assumed he had been dismissed as well. He bowed again and had turned to leave when Komodo stopped him. "No. Not you, General. You stay."

Komodo did not speak again until the room was empty. The vast room seemed even bigger when it was empty of people. Komodo lazed back on a pile of pillows, regarding his second in command critically for a moment or two.

"Tell me, Grillo . . . can I survive here when I destroy the last Lifespring in Tao?" His tone of voice was conversational, almost as if he were putting a philosophical question to his aide.

"No, my lord," Grillo replied dutifully.

"Now . . . ," he continued, "do you expect me to stay in a world where I cannot survive?"

Grillo shook his head slowly. "No, my lord. Of course not . . ." If he was wondering what he would do when the last Lifespring in Tao was no more, he gave no sign.

"No," Komodo repeated. "Of course not . . . You see, Grillo, when one has everything, desires are left unsatisfied. But there are other worlds— worlds where power and desire have no limits whatsoever. And this Manuscript will bring us to that other world. Do you understand?"

He nodded slightly. "I do not understand why you need this child, the Newcomer."

"He is the teller of tales," said Komodo. His

face hardened. "Go and find him, General Grillo."

Grillo bowed low. "I swear to you, My Lord, the Newcomer will be yours." He backed away from the bed and then turned toward the door. Komodo began to laugh.

"Oh, General . . ."

Grillo stopped. "Yes, my lord?"

"Do you think purple becomes me?"

"Purple, my lord?"

"Purple . . ." Komodo held one of the silk cushions against his chest. It was a deep, rich purple in color. "The color of royalty."

"Yes, my lord," Grillo replied.

"Then you are dismissed," said Komodo archly.

Grillo could hear Komodo's mad laughter echoing after him as he walked to the door.

THE VILLAGERS HAD GONE TO BED HAPPILY, SLEEPING A little more secure in their beds that night, safe and confident of their future, now that the Warriors of Virtue had been reunited at long last.

The five Rooz, still gathered at the Council Round, were less sure of the future, though they had been careful to conceal their doubts from the townsfolk. But now they were alone with Ryan— not even Master Chung was there—and they discussed what they should do in hushed tones, keeping their voices low so as not to be overheard.

"We have to go get the Manuscript," Chi declared firmly. "It's as simple as that."

"I promised Master Chung," said Yun, nodding. "I have sworn to get the Manuscript."

"Then we have to go at once!" said Chi, his voice rising a little. "There is no time to wait."

"Shouldn't we tell Master Chung what we're doing?" Tsun looked very doubtful. "We should do that at least."

"There is no time," said Chi vehemently. "Komodo's army is ready to attack!"

"Master Chung has said that we must be patient," Tsun said. "He advised caution."

"Patience is *not* my virtue," said Chi through gritted teeth. "You should know that by now."

"Yun," said Lai, "if all of us go, there will be chaos. Some of us will have to stay here."

"I made a pledge to these people," said Tsun solemnly. "I'm not going to leave them defenseless. We cannot do that. It would not be fair. And it wouldn't be prudent."

Yun looked at each of them in turn, then sighed. "I made a vow too, Tsun," he said. "*I* let the Manuscript fall into Komodo's hands. And *I* made the pledge to Master Chung. I will go myself."

Before Yun could say another word, Yee stood up and joined him, his arms crossed on his chest. He looked extremely resolute. There was no mistaking his gesture—he would go with Yun and he would brook no interference on the subject.

Then Chi rose. "And I'm with you two as well."

"What about me?" Ryan said as he scrambled to his feet. "I mean, Master Chung said I was the only one who could read the Manuscript. I have to go along then, right?"

The looks on the faces of the Rooz proclaimed that they had finally found an issue they could all agree on. All of them knew the grave dangers to be faced and not one of them wanted Ryan to go along on the expedition. The risks were too great.

Chi knelt down, until he was eye to eye with Ryan. "That would be most unwise," he said softly.

"But—"

Yee nodded too, and made some quick, soft gestures with his hands, like sign language.

"What did he say?" Ryan asked.

Chi translated for him. "He said that we cannot let anything happen to you. You are our friend, Ryan."

Ryan felt a stab of emotion and a lump in his throat. He put out his hand to Yee. "Shake?" he said.

Yee put out his own paw tentatively, not quite

sure what to do. Handshaking was not a tradition among the Roos.

"No," said Ryan. "Like this." Ryan showed him the special handshake he shared with the people closest to him. "See? Over, then under. Yeah! That's it. *Friends*."

12

RYAN AND THE ROOZ THOUGHT MASTER CHUNG WAS asleep in his hut on the edge of the village, but they were wrong. Deep in the night, the old man sat quietly on a mat on the floor, meditating on the events of the day. As he thought, turning the incidents over in his mind, he played absent-mindedly with a strand of smooth, cool jade beads.

The sudden appearance of Ryan and the Manu-script, the reunion of the Warriors of Virtue—these were miracles that could only have been sent to combat the evil plans of Komodo and his legions.

But Master Chung knew that there were great dangers and trials ahead. Even with the Manuscript and the one person who could read it, and with the reunited Rooz on their side, Komodo would be a difficult foe to vanquish. He commanded so many men, he had such immense power . . . But more than that, Komodo's mind was a trap, a twisted maze that could absorb people, power, concepts. He could bend other men to his will, even get them to act against their own interests—and to work for him.

As Master Chung thought, the twine holding the beads together parted and suddenly the beads spilled across the wooden floor of the hut. He watched as the beads clattered and scattered, a look of grave concern on his face. It was a sign, a bad omen . . .

RYAN WAS ASLEEP, WORN OUT BY THE AMAZING EVENTS OF the day. The instant Tsun had showed him to his bed in Yun's hut, he had collapsed and fallen into a deep sleep.

It was not, however, an untroubled sleep. He was lost in a dream and he thrashed in his sleep, getting twisted in the bedclothes, a low moan coming from his lips.

It was a bright, bright day in his dream and he was back in the real world. He was dressed in a football uniform and he had the ball tucked under his arm and was blasting up the field. The opposing team's goal line was in sight, but the defensemen seemed to be everywhere. He zigged and zagged, his feet pounding on the turf, his legs working like pistons as he broke through the waves of tacklers.

Ryan could hear the crowd. They were on their feet, screaming and hollering, yelling his name at the top of their lungs. Quickly it developed into a chant: "RY-AN! RY-AN! RY-*AN!*"

He could see his mom and dad in the stands—Mom was leaping with delight. Tracy was jumping up and down, joining in the chant. Then, just before he crossed the goal line, Ryan dropped the ball. Instantly, he was swarmed by the opposing team, who picked up the fumble and ran for the opposite end zone.

Then he woke up.

Ryan awoke with a start, dripping with sweat. Immediately he checked his leg to see if it still worked. He flexed it and bent it and was relieved to see that one thing, at least, was not just a dream.

Then he remembered where he was, and all that had happened to him that day. Ryan sighed heavily and lay back in the bed. The night was still and quiet. He rolled over on his stomach, his head on the edge of the bed. Then he noticed the slightest shimmer of silver, something protruding from beneath the bed. His curiosity piqued,

Ryan reached under and hauled it out. It was a long silk sack—and it contained an exquisite sword, a beautifully worked blade that shone like crystal in the moonlight.

"Wow," Ryan breathed.

"I wouldn't touch that if I was you."

Ryan jumped and whipped round, just in time to see Mudlap climbing through the window of the hut. The weird little creature slipped off the sill and landed on the floor with a thump.

"You!" said Ryan. "What are you doing here?"

Mudlap ignored the question. He pointed at the bundle in Ryan's hands. "That's Yun's sword you got there. Nobody touches Yun's sword, you know? Not even Yun anymore." He smiled a nasty little smile, showing a mouth full of crooked teeth. "Know what I mean?"

"You again. What do you want?" said Ryan. He got out of bed and leaned over the little man. After being around the towering Rooz, it was a relief to be bigger than someone.

"I got a deal for you, Newcomer," Mudlap said quickly. "I've got something you're looking for. Something you want real bad."

Ryan looked at Mudlap skeptically. Maybe he hadn't been in Tao very long, but he knew this strange creature was definitely bad news. "What have you got?"

"I'm not telling you till I get something in

return, Newcomer," said Mudlap. "What do you think I am? Stupid?"

Ryan grabbed Mudlap by the scruff of his neck and shook him roughly. "Tell me!"

Mudlap struggled frantically, desperate to get away. But Ryan held him tight. "Whoa! Whoa! Hold it! Okay, okay. Relax, I'll tell you, Newcomer, I'll tell you!"

"Okay. Tell me." Ryan let the little guy go and Mudlap straightened his clothing, as if trying to straighten his dignity.

"I've got the Manuscript," Mudlap said.

"You've got what?" Ryan's voice was as clear and as loud as a shout in the still night.

"Ssshhhhhh," said Mudlap, waving his hands. "Yeah. I've got it. I stole it out from under Komodo's nose."

"Show it to me," Ryan ordered.

Mudlap did a double take and looked at Ryan as if he had suddenly taken leave of his senses.

"Are you crazy?" Mudlap asked. "I don't have it here. I got it hid. Hid where no one is going to find it either. But I'll take you to where I got it stashed, okay?"

"No!" said Ryan excitedly. "We have to get Master Chung. We have to tell the others!"

"No, no, no," said Mudlap quickly. "You ain't listenin' to me, Newcomer. The Manuscript ain't theirs! Is it? No! It's *yours*. And once they use up

165

all its power, how are you gonna get home? Huh? Did you ever think about that, Newcomer?"

Ryan squinted at the little man. In fact, he had not thought about how he was going to get home—so much had happened in such a short time, there had been no time to consider it really—and he had to admit that Mudlap made a little sense.

"See? You wanna stay here forever?" Mudlap asked, taunting Ryan. "Never see your family again? How about your friends? You'll never see them again either. The way I see it, it's now or never for you, Newcomer. If you want to get outta here, you're gonna have to go now. Right?"

Ryan struggled with himself. He could not stay in Tao forever, and if there was only one way out . . .

Then he thought about his newfound friends, how they had accepted him, how they were counting on him now. He had a skill that no one, not even Master Chung, possessed.

"I can't leave now," said Ryan passionately. "They need me here. They're *counting* on me."

Mudlap shrugged. "Hey, that's fine with me, Newcomer. You don't want it, I'll go and offer it to someone else. A lot of people around here want that Manuscript, you know." He shrugged again and then he started to climb up toward the window again.

"Wait!" said Ryan. "Wait just a minute."

Mudlap grinned his nasty little smile again. "I knew you'd see it my way, Newcomer. But if you want it . . ." Mudlap turned and jumped down from the windowsill.

"What?"

Mudlap rubbed his fingers together rapidly. "I need a small reward for my efforts."

"I don't have—" Then Ryan removed the watch on his wrist and handed it to Mudlap. "Here, take it."

"What is it?" Mudlap asked suspiciously as he took the watch from Ryan.

"It's a watch," said Ryan. "It's a good one."

Mudlap held it under his nose and sniffed it, then put it between his yellow teeth and bit it. "I guess it's better than nothing. Now, follow me."

He darted up to the window and was through it in a flash. Ryan squeezed through after him . . .

THERE WAS ALMOST NO LIGHT IN KOMODO'S BEDROOM; a single lamp burning cast a feeble beam on the vast bed. There was a figure approaching the bed, a woman—but it wasn't one of the ones who had been there earlier. This one was taller, with long, golden hair and deep blue eyes. It was Elysia. But her beautiful face was drawn in guilt.

"Your guilt is obscene," said Komodo nastily. "*It was a life!* You must learn to yield to vengeance."

There were tears in Elysia's eyes and she was

stricken with humiliation at her betrayal. Then she caught sight of the object that Komodo held in his hands and her eyes glittered. It was a slim vial of Zubrium.

Komodo saw her interest and he sneered at her. "It must be time for your medication."

Elysia reached for the vial, but Komodo snatched it away. She lunged and he pulled it away again, toying with her, keeping it just beyond her reach. Komodo put the bed between them.

"This Newcomer," he said, "I gather he has taken a liking to you. Is that true?"

"Yes, Komodo," she said. Her eyes did not leave the little tube of the Zubrium. Her hunger for it was obvious.

"And you care for him?" Komodo asked.

Elysia shrugged slightly. "The Newcomer has fallen under my spell, Komodo."

Komodo laughed and shook his head. "And a wicked little spell it is, Elysia." He reached out and caught her by the wrist, pulling her close, attempting to kiss her on the lips. But Elysia pulled back.

"What are you afraid of?" he said.

She went limp and stopped fighting him, allowing him a kiss in return for the vial of Zubrium.

"Afraid? I'm not afraid of you."

Elysia uncorked the tube of Zubrium and downed it like an addict. As the liquid flooded through her body, her eyes glittered. She seemed to change before Komodo's eyes, a small fiendish smile on her face. She was no longer the innocent, but had become, instead, the seductress.

And the metamorphosis seemed to amuse Komodo. "Elysia, you are such a wicked, *wicked* creature."

She came in close and permitted him to take her in his arms. "Really? Then what does that make you?"

"Lucky," he said. Then he kissed her deeply, crushing her slim body against his.

MUDLAP HAD LED RYAN DEEP INTO THE FOREST, FARTHER in than the boy had ever been before. The little creature was running along the footpaths, his short legs carrying him quickly—it was all Ryan could do to keep up with him.

"Come on! Come on!" Mudlap urged. "Hurry. You don't want to be out here all night, do you?"

Ryan was not watching where he was going— he probably could not find his way back if his life depended on it. All he wanted to do was get his hands on that Manuscript and get it into Master Chung's hands. Ryan was sure that the wise old man would know what to do with it—surely there had to be a way to use the Manuscript to defeat Komodo and the legions, as well as a way to send Ryan back to the real world.

But then—everything changed. As Ryan raced

down the path, General Grillo stepped out from the trees, blocking his way. He grabbed Ryan and held him tightly.

"Hey!" Ryan yelped.

"Sorry, Newcomer," Mudlap giggled. "Nothing personal about this, you understand."

Grillo dropped a couple of shiny stones into Mudlap's grimy hands. "Thank you, General Grillo," he said as he snuck off into the night. "Virtue be yours."

"Jerk!" Ryan spat after him.

Grillo smiled. "Welcome to the other side, Newcomer." His grip on the boy seemed to tighten and he started to drag him down the path. But suddenly, a breeze picked up, a wind wafting through the trees, blowing dust from the forest floor into Grillo's eyes.

Grillo rubbed the grit from his eyes—and when he opened them, Master Chung was standing there, a small stick in his hands. Grillo went for his sword, but Master Chung swatted him lightly with the small switch, a brief tap that temporarily paralyzed the general. His tight grip on Ryan relaxed and he broke free.

"Grillo," said Master Chung. "This is not your way." Master Chung sounded disappointed that General Grillo had stooped as low as kidnapping to achieve his aims.

Ryan hid behind Master Chung and watched,

amazed at what might happen next. Grillo was staring at the master helplessly.

"Komodo's lies are blinding your vision, General Grillo. The truth is still there." He tapped his own chest. "It is still in your heart."

The spell was broken. Grillo pulled a vial of Zubrium from his tunic and downed it. It had the same effect on the general that it had on Elysia. He seemed strengthened, rejuvenated—and with evil in his eyes.

"Komodo offers more than you ever did, Chung." He felt the Zubrium in his veins and reached for his sword to deal a death blow to Master Chung once and for all.

But then the color drained from General Grillo's face. Master Chung and Ryan had vanished . . .

13

KOMODO'S THRONE ROOM WAS DESERTED AND BATHED IN eerie shadows and silence. Stealthily, the Rooz crept into the room—it was surprising that creatures so large could move with such surreptitiousness and grace. They scarcely made a sound.

The manuscript was just where Komodo had left it—on the plinth in front of the overblown throne. Yun was just about to reach for it when Chi put out a hand to stop him.

"No, wait," he hissed. "It can't be as easy as this. There must be some kind of alarm or security. That's how Komodo thinks. He wouldn't just leave it here." He peered closely at the pedestal, as did the other Rooz. But there was nothing.

But Yee, always impatient, just grabbed the Manuscript. But the instant he got it, the Manuscript vanished, and there was a loud explosion followed by the clanking sound of machinery. Chains shot from the walls, wrapping around the Rooz and cuffing them tightly at the wrists and ankles.

Almost instantly, the chains were retracted on counterweights, throwing the Rooz into the air and stringing them up helplessly. Their arms and legs were spread, their tails whipping this way and that as they struggled against the bonds that held them so securely.

A split second later the tall throne room doors burst open and Mantose, Dullard and Barbarocious burst into the chamber, while dozens of Dragoon soldiers poured in behind them.

When Mantose caught sight of the Rooz, he cackled loudly and pointed. "Got you! Got you!"

Dullard and Barbarocious hissed and giggled, jumping up and down like a pair of lunatics. The soldiers giggled too, laughing at the hapless Rooz, taunting them mercilessly.

"Nice going, Yee," Chi said.

Yee did his best to shrug, as if to say, *Those are the breaks—these things happen.*

Then Elysia swept into the room and gazed up at the Rooz. For a moment they had no idea what she was doing there—had she been captured too?—but then she started to laugh. It was mean, nasty, slightly hysterical laughter, as if she had to laugh louder than anyone to prove that she had changed sides, that she was not one of them—not anymore.

"Oh, Rooooooz," she sneered. "Protectors of the Tao . . . protectors of the weak and the vulnerable . . . the helpless."

Yun could not believe his eyes. "Elysia? Is that you?"

"Are you surprised, Yun?" she yelled. "You, the holder of the virtue of Benevolence—who kills. Enjoy your restitution."

Then came Komodo himself, striding into the throne chamber. He stopped at the threshold, laughed, then walked up to Elysia and took her hand, the two of them, lord and lady, prancing up to the Rooz.

"Glad you could hang around," Komodo brayed. Then he laughed loudly, cracking himself up. When the boss laughed, the rest of the room erupted in laughter too. Komodo circled the Rooz, taunting them, delighted to see his enemies trapped like this. He was playing to the crowd as if he was a performer on center stage.

"I have found the recipe for Roo stew," he announced with a cackle. "Simply chop the meat into several tiny pieces and mince, then sprinkle with a hint of Benevolence. Marinade in Wisdom for many, many years. Add just a touch of *Order!*"

At the sound of the last word, his soldiers and lieutenants snapped to attention.

"And let it simmer in Righteousness. It goes down well with a nice cold vial of . . ." he glanced at Elysia but wandered over to Barbarocious and bent down as if to kiss her. "Well, what else: Zubrium."

"You forgot Loyalty," Yun shouted.

But Komodo decided against kissing his female lieutenant. "Oh, but Loyalty only last so long . . . It spoils." This time he kissed Elysia. Barbra-Rotious did not like this at all and she glared at her, then scraped her long fingernails on the granite floor. Yun and the rest of the Rooz were horrified to see Komodo kissing their Elysia.

"Chi," said Komodo. "I am surprised . . . Your foolishness astonishes me. You come uninvited into my home, being the animals that you are." He glanced toward the door. "And like animals I will serve you up as a stew to my dear friend and much honored guest, the Newcomer."

General Grillo was standing in the doorway, but it took a moment for everyone to realize that the general did not have the Newcomer with him. The cheering stopped abruptly. There was a taut moment of silence. Then Komodo took a step closer. It was apparent to everyone in the room, the Rooz included, that the general was so scared he was trembling.

"Where is he?" Komodo demanded.

"I don't have him," said Grillo, almost choking on the words. He looked scared and miserable.

"What happened?" Komodo demanded. "Where is the Newcomer, General Grillo?"

"He escaped," the general said miserably.

"*How?*"

"It was Chung."

Komodo looked taken aback by this piece of information. "It was Chung, you say?" Then Komodo did something no one expected him to do. He smiled. Then he turned to the Rooz, facing them now with an even greater air of invincibility.

"That's good, General Grillo . . . Very good." He smacked his lips. "That's tasty. I'll add a dash of the old man to the dish . . . and I'll enjoy your Lifespring for dessert."

"No!" Yun shouted. He strained with every muscle in his body to try and break his bonds, but it was plain that the chains were far too strong to be broken.

Komodo snapped his fingers. "General Grillo."

The general stepped forward. He knew what he was supposed to do. Recessed into the wall was a black metal lever. Grillo yanked it back to the sound of grinding gears. Instantly, the section of the floor beneath the Rooz slid back, revealing a churning steel chute and, at the bottom of that, wide, sharp blades spinning like a propeller.

Komodo turned to Elysia, expecting to see her looking as delighted as he was. But instead, she was looking up at the Rooz, a faint look of remorse at what she had done pressed into her pretty face.

"What are you waiting for?" Komodo asked. He pointed to the lever in General Grillo's hand. "Do it now."

But Elysia did not move. Komodo leaned over her shoulder and whispered in her ear. "Betrayal gets easier with time, Elysia," he said. "Believe me, I know what I'm talking about."

Still, Elysia did not move. Her eyes were locked on Yun's and she could see the hurt there. Komodo took her hand and started to lead her out of the room, leaving the Rooz to their grisly fates.

"Drop them, General," he ordered.

Before he could act, Yun shouted out, his voice filling the vast chamber. "Is it worth it, Grillo?"

General Grillo gripped the lever tight, but something stopped him from pulling it. He, like Elysia, looked up at Yun.

"General Grillo," said Komodo sternly. "Do your duty please."

"You belong with us," Yun yelled. "Like it used to be with us. Remember? When we were young! You can't have forgotten about those days, Grillo!"

Grillo needed a quick fortifying gulp of Zubrium from the cylinder in his belt. "Remember? I remember it well, Yun. It's you who have forgotten the past. You forget that we played on opposite sides even back then when we were children."

"We were still friends," Yun shouted. "That means something. Even from so long ago."

Grillo winced, as if he had been pinched. He stared up into Yun's eyes. For a moment, there was a flicker of compassion—but it didn't last for longer than a moment or two. Komodo's booming voice thundered through the room, shaking it like a ton of dynamite, a cannonlike roar that shook the entire chamber to the foundations.

"Drop them!"

General Grillo shuddered with such fear that his hand worked the lever out of the pure instinct of self-defense. He yanked on the lever and the chains released the Rooz, dropping them straight into the churning chute. The floor closed over them with a noisy clang.

Grillo merely stood there, staring with vacant eyes at the closed death chute. Dullard, Mantose and Barbarocious just laughed at him, cackling with manic glee.

"Good . . . very good" said Komodo evenly. "Now . . . I think we have some work to do."

*　　*　　*

AT FIRST, NO ONE NOTICED—EVERYONE IN THE VILLAGE was still sleeping. The sound was far off, on the horizon. The sound of men on the march—Dragoon soldiers.

Then the ground began to tremble slightly, and then it intensified. By the time the villagers around the Lifespring had awoken and rubbed the sleep from their eyes, they were under attack.

From the dusty, dry vapors of Komodo's wasteland, his army had swept into the Radius of Green, then bore down on the Lifespring, determined, this time, to destroy it.

Mantose was at the head of a platoon of forty men, but as they charged into the perimeter of the Lifespring, the ground in front of them began to move. Then, all of a sudden, the ground opened up and Tsun sprung up from under a cover of grass and dirt.

Mantose was thrown back as Tsun attacked. She advanced, throwing out a dizzying flurry of hits and kicks. She spun, she jabbed, she kicked—each hit landing precisely, jarring blows that flattened each soldier she struck. Mantose snarled and fought back, but Tsun refused to give ground, her ears folding down in determination as more soldiers came at her.

Dullard brought one of his own squads of Dragoon soldiers across one of the footbridges. Villagers rushed to engage them, but they were no match for the Dragoon soldiers. The few men and women who had managed to get out of bed in time to repel the invaders fought as best they could, but the Dragoon soldiers were hardened, merciless men. And they showed no mercy then, slashing and striking out.

Then Lai stepped into the fray, evening the odds a little. Without warning he dropped from the tree limbs above, challenging Dullard directly. He spun in a fast, tight circle, his staff held out, knocking soldiers flying. He planted himself firmly and challenged the next wave. There were a lot of soldiers—too many of them.

Lai did not feel fear, but he did feel a certain disgust for the men who had suddenly invaded the peaceful village and its Lifespring.

"Mayhem!" he said in disgust. "Pure mayhem!

14

THE ONLY SOUNDS IN THE DEATH CHUTE WERE THE whispering of the blades and the heavy breathing of the Rooz. It was pitch dark in the shaft and none of the Rooz were quite sure what had happened once they had been dropped in there. All they could really be sure of was that they had not been sliced and diced by the razor-sharp blades—not yet anyway.

"Chi," Yun gasped in the darkness. "Give us some light."

Suddenly, a flame flared, a single orange tongue dancing on the end of Chi's thumb. Much of the chute was in dark shadow, but there was enough light to get an idea of what had happened to them.

Yun had managed to loop a rope over one of the short blades that lined the interior of the channel blades. Chi had a single arm around Yun's waist and Yee was holding on to Chi's feet, his metal rings dangling. On either side of them was the thicket of knives protruding from the walls—if they moved one inch to the right or left they would be impaled and sliced to ribbons.

The weight of the three of them on the rope was too much. Slowly, but surely, the sharp blade was slicing through the strands—soon it would give way and drop them to the huge fan blades at the bottom of the shaft. Beyond that was a burning pool of hot oil. Yee began to struggle, as if he were trying to fight his way back up the chute.

"Yee!" Yun ordered, his voice bouncing off the steel walls. "Do not panic!"

But in that moment, the rope gave way and the three Rooz plunged toward the rotating bands of razor-sharp metal. As they tumbled, Yee whipped a ring from his tunic and threw it at the spinning blades, but it merely bounced off and whipped back up the shaft.

Running on pure instinct, Yun threw out a hand and grabbed one of the knives on the wall, snatching at Chi's tail with the other hand. In the same moment, Chi grabbed Yee's tail—stopping Yee's face just inches from the rotating fan blades.

Yun knew he couldn't hold on for long—the knife cut his flesh and the pain was excruciating.

"Chi," he gasped, fighting back the pain in his hand. "Can you throw one of the rings?"

Chi nodded and pulled another steel circlet from his belt. He licked his lips and concentrated, throwing the thick loop directly at the mechanism that powered the rotating steel. This time the ring found its mark, jamming itself between the blades, stopping them in mid sweep.

The Rooz dropped down onto the blades, the pool of fire roaring just beneath their feet. The moving parts of the death chute groaned and creaked, churning and moaning, straining against the puny metal ring that held them in check. The blades were moving slightly, slowly crushing the loop. They did not have much time—a few seconds at best.

"There has to be a way out of here!" Yun scanned the walls at the base of the shaft and found what he was looking for. There was a panel set in the wall and he kicked it in with one savage blow. He didn't know what it was—work shaft or ventilation channel—and he didn't care. But it was a way out.

"This way!"

Chi went fist, sliding down the secondary shaft quickly, followed a moment later by Yun. Then it was Yee's turn, but being the biggest of the Rooz, he found it a tight fit—he was stuck.

Yun and Chi grabbed handfuls of Yee's fur and tried to pull him down, but he wouldn't budge. Yee's head was still sticking into the death chute, and as soon as the rig gave way, the blades would sweep around and cut it off. He felt a panic rising inside of him and he started to struggle, attempting to force his way down the escape chute.

"Yee, calm yourself," said Yun, doing his best to stay calm himself. "Calm yourself, like water. Take a deep breath."

Yee's huge lungs inflated, then he exhaled quickly—and slipped down the shaft.

They were outdoors somewhere—none of them knew where—but they were alive and they knew that their Lifespring was under attack. There was no time to lose. Yee was a little annoyed—Yun and Chi had pulled so hard that he had lost a tuft of fur. Still, it was a small price to pay—the alternative could have been so much worse.

IN CONTRAST TO THE REST OF TAO, THE RUINS OF THE OLD temple in the ancient Rooz village was peaceful and quiet. Master Chung and Ryan sat next to a small fire, the orange light reflecting off their faces.

"Will the Manuscript really be able to get me home?" Ryan asked. "Does it have that power?"

Master Chung nodded slowly. "Yes," he said. "It has the power to help us all, Ryan."

"What about my leg?" Ryan asked eagerly. "Does it have the power to keep it the way it is now—not the way it was before." He had been without a limp for only a few hours, but even now he could not imagine going back to the old way of living.

Master Chung looked at Ryan, a thoughtful smile on his old, lined features. "What matters is not what you gain here," he pointed at Ryan's leg, "but what you gain here." He closed his hands over his own heart. "That is what you must learn."

Ryan looked at him for a moment, tears welling up in his eyes. "But I want it to be strong. I want it to stay the way it is now. Why did it have to be like this anyway? Why did it have to happen to *me*."

"Every person has a weakness, Ryan," said Master Chung. "A defect, an imperfection. Maybe you don't always see them, but they are there. Overcoming them is the true test of strength."

"But my leg just *is*. It just is like that. I didn't have anything to do with it. I'd do anything to make it strong." He shrugged his shoulders, miserably. "But it just *is* . . ."

"Do you consider the Warriors of Virtue to be strong?" Master Chung asked him.

"Well, yeah," said Ryan with another shrug. "Look at 'em . . ."

Master Chung shook his head. "No. That is not correct. The strength they have is not what you see. You cannot see the strength of them. It is their virtue. *That* is their Kung."

Ryan looked puzzled. "Kung? What's Kung?"

"Have you never wondered, Ryan, what the words Kung Fu really mean?"

Ryan opened his mouth to answer that he knew exactly what Kung Fu meant, then realized that he did not. Not literally, not precisely . . . "I don't know, Master Chung. I thought I did. But now I'm not so sure. What's the Kung part?"

The old man smiled. "Kung is your energy, your inner strength," Master Chung explained. "It can be positive or negative. Those like Komodo use Negative Kung to kill and destroy.

"Komodo is very, very powerful, but he thinks that his power belongs to him, that only he can possess it. To share is to be defeated. The true way, the way of virtue, is a much easier path to follow than the one Komodo has chosen. But yet he follows that difficult one. Look at how he lives—in a great fortress, with soldiers killing for him, with slaves dying for him . . . Is he happier than the lowliest person in this village? No. He lives in fear. He knows his own evil and fears that there may be a greater evil out there, one that could vanquish him."

"But what about the other Kung?" Ryan asked. "The kind that isn't evil. The kind that you and the Rooz have."

"Ah," said Master Kung, smiling warmly. "That is the most important thing. If you bring your virtues together within you, you will create Positive Kung. With that alone, you will always have the power to do the right thing. Summon up the positive, the virtuous, and you will be able to do anything. You will read the Manuscript of Legend."

Ryan stared at the old man for a moment, trying to make sense of his words. Then he nodded.

"But . . . if no one else can read the Manuscript, how will I be able to read it?"

"The answer lies within you," said Master Chung. "You have to find it inside."

"But—" Ryan wanted to know more, but he could tell by the expression on Master Chung's face that something had happened, from one second to another, something had changed. It was as if he sensed something—something evil, something ominous. The old man leaned down, reaching for a long blade of straw, whispering to Ryan as he bent over.

"Ryan . . . when I tell you to run, follow that path and go." He nodded toward a path through the ruins and into the trees. "Don't stop running until you get to the Lifespring."

"Huh? What are you—"

Then Komodo stepped out of the shadows. Ryan had never seen the overlord, but he did not have to be told who it was—and he was frozen by his first glimpse of the evil man.

"Run!"

RYAN TURNED AND RAN, RACING FOR THE PATH. THE instant he was off, though, Komodo flew into the air to intercept him. But Chung, with the skill of the ages, threw himself into the air and the two men crashed and fell—but they were on their feet in a split second.

They faced each other, circling, each man looking for the other's weakness, the place to press the attack. Master Chung had nothing in his hands but the stalk he had plucked from the ground but Komodo carried a massive, wicked sword in his gloved hands.

Komodo sneered at the old master. "Is that your only weapon, Chung? What is it, the last straw?"

Komodo did not know it, but that piece of straw had already drawn blood. Just above Komodo's cheek, a trace of blood appeared from a small, paper-thin cut. He touched the cut gingerly—he saw the blood on his fingers and his eyes grew wide with anger.

"All right, old man!" Komodo shrieked madly. "Your time has come at long last."

The two supreme masters tangled in a majestic display of Kung Fu. They flew through the air, smashing from tree to tree, rock to rock, branch to branch. The old stone walls of the ruins exploded from the impact of the two battling champions. There was no doubt that this was the ultimate clash between these two old enemies—a struggle that could only be a battle to the death.

Ryan had not done what Master Chung had told him to do. Instead of running all the way back to the Lifespring as the master had ordered, he had just darted into the forest, then burrowed into a hollowed-out log to watch the outcome of the battle between Master Chung and Komodo.

He never saw it. No sooner had he crawled into the log, than Barbarocious's head appeared at the opening, cackling wildly. Her long, clammy tongue snaked out of her mouth and swiped across his face.

"Oh! Gross!" Ryan screamed. He shimmied out of the log and ran back the way he had come, Barbarocious shrieking behind him like a banshee.

Ryan burst into the clearing where the battle was still going on. "Master Chung!" Ryan yelped.

Still parrying his opponent's attacks, Master Chung glanced quickly at Ryan. So did Komodo. Suddenly there was a pause, a moment of decision in the midst of the fierce battle, action and deliberation balanced on a razor's edge, both men weighing their chances and calculating the price of victory. And then the moment passed, and Komodo feinted toward Ryan, and Master Chung threw himself in front of the boy. There was murderous triumph in Komodo's eyes as he brought his sword across in a vicious arc, generating a sheet of Negative Kung, a burst of hot red energy. The Kung entered Chung and blew out the front of his body, the force of the power exploding the ruined walls that fenced them in.

Rocks and debris rained out of the dark sky. Chung dropped to his knees, his face frozen, his eyes on Ryan. It was plain that a death blow had been struck and Ryan watched horrified, sure that he could almost see the life flowing from the old man's broken body.

But there was something wrong with Komodo as well. He was short of breath and on his knees, struggling to crawl the few feet to where Master Chung lay, straining to look into the old man's face. The life was fluttering inside Master Chung's breast like a bird in a cage.

"I'll ask you one more time, old man," Komodo gasped, his voice hoarse, strained and weak. "And this time you have give me the answer. This hell is my prison. Tell me . . . tell me, what will set me free."

Master Chung gazed at Komodo with something like forgiveness in his old eyes. "The only hell in this world, Komodo, is in your heart. That is where all battles must be fought."

Those were his last words. Imparting his last piece of wisdom to the man who had killed him, Master Chung gave up his soul, closing his eyes and dying there in the clearing.

Ryan was too stunned to move. At first he could not quite believe what had happened—that Master Chung had been vanquished. In the world of a twelve-year-old, good always triumphed over evil. Men like Komodo could never prevail against a man like Master Chung.

He was staring at Komodo and he knew he had to run, to escape, but he was rooted to the spot. He had never felt more terrified.

"You are not going anywhere," said Komodo. "Do you understand me, Newcomer?"

Finally, Ryan got himself to move. He turned and fled—and ran right into the arms of Barbarocious.

15

Tsun and Lai were surrounded. They fought back-to back, dispatching any Dragoon soldier who dared to get within range of their iron-hard hands and vicious kicks. But they were weakening—even the Rooz had finite amounts of energy—slowly becoming worn down by the brutal battle. Every muscle in their bodies ached and they were bleeding from a dozen cuts and gashes. They would fight on until the last breath in their bodies, but both of them knew the sad facts— they were losing.

Dullard moved in for the kill, launching one of his evil steel darts at Lai. He blocked it with the shaft of his wooden flute, catching the dart in mid-flight. Then he twirled the flute in his fingers, put the mouthpiece of the instrument to his lips and blew a blast of air into it. The dart shot out of the flute as if from a peashooter and zoomed back at Dullard, striking him in the chest and knocking him flat.

But Dullard's men still came—a dozen or more Dragoon soldiers advancing on Tsun and Lai. The numbers were just too overwhelming— there was nothing that could be done. Though they fought on, Tsun and Lai knew that even Master Chung would counsel flight when the odds against them were so monumental.

Lai tried to drag Tsun away from the fight but she would not budge. "Tsun! Come on! There are too many of them."

Tsun felled a soldier with a savage blow—no soft fist here, not now—and refused to budge.

"No," she shouted. "You go."

"Don't be—" Lai realized that words would have no affect on her. He grabbed her by the sleeve and leaped, carrying her away from the battle and into the branches of the trees above them. He hooked a vine in one hand and with the other grasped Tsun, pushing them out into space. They swung in a wide arc, from one vine to the next, escaping the soldiers swarming like bees on the ground below them.

Throughout the village, fighting had already

come to an end. Villagers who had not fallen to the soldiers had realized the futility of further resistance and surrendered. These hapless people were clapped into heavy chains and taken away like slaves, under heavy guard.

The rest of the soldiers—hundreds of them—tore through the village, methodically stripping the little settlement of anything of value. Others put boats on the lake, hacking through the Zubrium savagely and dropping wide-mouthed hoses into the clear water to pump the mineral from the Lifespring. They worked hard, as if determined to kill the Lifespring as quickly and as brutally as possible, as if they hated this beautiful place.

Yun, Chi and Yee crept as close as they dared to the edge of the village, peering down into the settlement from the heights above the lake, their hearts sinking as they watched the despoiling of their little hamlet. The three Rooz were numb, realizing that there was nothing they could do to stop the violation of the Lifespring.

"We have to find the others," Chi whispered. "Tsun and Lai would not have allowed themselves to be taken."

"Where can they be?" said Yun, his voice hollow and grim. He was too stunned by what was unfolding in front of his eyes to allow himself to think with clarity.

"There's still a place that's safe," said Chi. "Come on . . ."

DEEP IN THE UNDERBELLY OF KOMODO'S FORTRESS, THE newly made slaves were forced to process the newly taken Zubrium. The Zubrium was loaded into the huge pendulums anchored in the walls, then swung toward the daylight, sending bright white shafts into the upper reaches of the fortress.

The mixture of Zubrium and light was funneled into Komodo's throne room and he sat in the stream of life-giving light, still as a lizard on a flat rock. His skin drank in the mixture, absorbing it like a drug.

There was very little light in the chamber adjoining Komodo's bedroom. Ryan was shoved in there by two Dragoon soldiers, then left alone. He looked with little interest at the amber-colored ceiling and at the spectacular bed that hung suspended from the ceiling. He had seen and heard too much during his time in Tao. Nothing could surprise him . . .

Nothing, that is, until Elysia swept into the room. Her simple clothing was gone, replaced by an extravagant gown, her face heavily made up, her beautiful hair teased and combed, piled on her head. He hardly recognized her—and he knew, instantly, what had happened.

"Elysia . . . ," he said in disbelief. "What's going on? What are you doing?" He backed away as she approached him, as if afraid that her touch would contaminate him.

"Ryan . . . I wanted to tell you," she said, pleading with him, a beseeching look in her eyes. "I couldn't tell you . . . Not at the beginning . . . Not at first . . ."

Ryan continued to back away from her. "Tell me what? That you're on *his* side? That you're a traitor? No . . ."

Elysia raised her hands; her nails had been painted a shade of bloody red. "Please . . . Let me explain."

"*No!*" Ryan yelled, his voice bouncing off the hard, flat planes of the walls. "Master Chung is dead! How could you do this to them? They protected you."

Elysia's lovely features changed, twisting into a sneer. Anger blazed in her blue eyes. "Protect? With that creed of theirs? The creed not to kill? But they did kill! Yun killed!"

"But . . . but he killed one of the bad guys!" Ryan insisted. "Sometimes it happens."

"But it was my brother!" Elysia cried passionately. "It happened to my brother." There was so much pain and misery in her voice Ryan could only stare at her for a moment, taken aback by this stunning revelation. She looked brokenhearted, torn apart both by the death of her beloved brother and by her own betrayal of the people she loved.

"No!" said Ryan. "I don't believe you! It couldn't have been like that. You're lying to me."

Elysia shook her head slowly. "No . . . no, I'm not . . ." She shrugged. "Of course, it doesn't matter now. It's all over for them. Finished . . . Yun and the others are dead. Komodo killed them. But now you have the chance to go home. You should take it."

News of the death of the Rooz was like a burning dagger in Ryan's chest. "Shut up! Just shut up!" he yelled, storming around the room. "You set me up, Elysia. And you said you were my friend!"

"Ryan, I know you don't believe this . . . but I *am* your friend," she said softly. "And I beg you. Do what Komodo wants. I don't want you to be hurt. Do what he says. Please . . ."

Ryan ran from her, but suddenly Komodo stepped out from one of the columns, scaring him half to death.

Ryan screamed and then stopped running, frozen in fear. Komodo strolled up to him, as if he had not a care in the world. As he came closer, Ryan could see that he carried something in his hands. It was the electronic football game from Ryan's backpack.

Komodo showed him the game, then looked down at the playing field, his fingers working magic on the small device.

"I've gotten quite good at playing with this.

Foot . . . ball. Correct?" Komodo scored a touchdown and a musical tone emanated from the game. "It's a pretty simple game really," he said. Then he looked at Ryan, directly. It felt as if someone had turned a searchlight on him. "Tell me, are you any good at football, Newcomer?"

Ryan did his best to resist the dominating force of Komodo's intense personality.

"You . . . you don't know anything about me, Komodo," he said. "You couldn't know."

"Oh, but I do," Komodo replied, his voice low and seductive. "I know your sorrow. And I embrace your loneliness. Look into my eyes, Ryan. See your desires. See everything you can become. I am your darkest thoughts. I am your friend. And I am proud to be your destiny . . ."

Ryan had been stunned into silence. He looked into the man's eyes as if looking into the mesmerizing eyes of a cobra. He could feel Komodo's eyes penetrating deep into his brain, as if they were feeling the same feelings, thinking the same thoughts.

Komodo pulled the manuscript from a fold in his cloak and showed it to him. "No one will ever laugh at you again," he said softly. "Let's go home . . . Ryan Jeffers. *With* your new leg. *Touchdown* . . ."

Ryan could feel the seductive power of evil creeping into him. He broke the gaze long enough to glance at Elysia.

"Do it, Ryan . . ."

Komodo put the Manuscript directly into Ryan's hands, leaning in closer, whispering. "In . . . or out?"

For a moment, Ryan could not react. Then, with trembling hands, he opened the book, turning to the first page. It was blank . . . He turned to the second page . . . It was blank too.

"Read it to me," Komodo ordered.

"Right," said Ryan. He felt a sickening feeling in the pit of his stomach and sweat was forming along his brow and upper lip. He riffled the pages—*all* of them were blank.

"Read!" Komodo commanded.

Ryan opened his mouth but before he could speak, General Grillo burst into the room.

"My lord," said Grillo. "Their Lifespring is in our control."

"I know that," said Komodo.

General Grillo hesitated for a split second before delivering his next piece of news. "But the Rooz have escaped," the General said nervously. "All of them."

"What!"

"I am sorry, my lord. They will be found."

Komodo's eyes burned with anger. He grabbed Ryan by the shoulder. "I will deal with that later. Now, Ryan—read."

Ryan stared at the pages, his brain working in overdrive. If the Rooz were alive as Grillo said, then there was a chance that they could still win, that Komodo could be defeated.

"In or out?" Komodo demanded.

Ryan glanced at Komodo, a serene calm in his eyes. "I'm in," he said evenly.

"Good. Now, what does it say?"

"It says . . ." *Think of something profound*, he told himself. "It says . . . Shit happens."

Komodo started as if he had been shocked or pinched, and stared hard at him.

"It says what?"

"It says 'shit happens.'"

"'Shit happens?'"

Ryan nodded. "Yeah. That's what it says."

"'Shit happens . . .'" Komodo considered this pithy aphorism for a moment. "Shit. Happens. All right . . . Keep reading."

His eyes darted toward the door, scouting an escape route. If he could get out of there, get back to the Rooz, then they could attempt a counterattack. He couldn't tell if Komodo was buying it. He was pacing the chamber, contemplating the words he had heard, mumbling them under his breath, nodding to himself as if it did, indeed, mean something.

While Komodo pondered the great truths suddenly revealed to him, Ryan edged toward the door. Komodo didn't notice this, but Elysia did. But she said nothing.

"'Shit happens. Don't worry, be happy.'"

Komodo stopped pacing and turned to face Ryan, his eyes like daggers penetrating his soul, like sharp, hot knives.

"You can't read it, can you?"

Ryan could not speak, but the color had drained from his face, giving Komodo all the answer he needed.

"Then you are nothing to me!" he screamed. He raised his hand to strike Ryan—a single blow from Komodo could kill—but Elysia caught his arm and held it.

"Please, Komodo! Don't do it!"

Suddenly, Elysia's intense eyes went blank, turning to a lifeless stare, as if a light had been snuffed out somewhere deep inside of her. A trickle of blood oozed from between her lips. Then Barbarocious stepped out from behind her, pulling her long fingernails from the woman's back. Blood flecked the palm of her hand.

"No one touches my master," Barbarocious whispered jealously. "No one."

As Elysia's body crumpled to the floor, Barbarocious looked over at Komodo, grinning seductively, running that long tongue over her lips. Komodo stepped over to her and gently cradled her head in his hands. Barbarocious looked as if she would pass out from the pleasure of her master's captivating touch.

"Barbarocious . . . ," Komodo murmured. "You are so . . . stupid!" He squeezed his hands

together and there was a sickening crack somewhere inside the evil woman's skull. She was
dead in an instant. Komodo let go of her head
and she tumbled to the floor, joining Elysia's
lifeless corpse sprawled on the cold black marble.

Komodo turned to Ryan once again. But Ryan
was gone.

"I want him alive!" Komodo roared. "Alive!"

16

RYAN HAD CHARGED OUT OF THE CHAMBER AND DOWN THE first set of steps he saw, running deep into the guts of the fortress. There was only one thing on his mind and that was escape—there had to be a way out of this nightmarish place somewhere. But the fortress was like a maze; he ran through room after room, each one larger than the last, and down a series of long dark corridors, until he was in the very underbelly of the fortress. He stopped at the intersection of two giant hallways and tried to accustom his eyes to the gloom. Deep down in the fortress was like being in some ugly mountain cave. The walls looked wet and slimy, the floors were slick with some kind of scum and black drops of foul water dripped from the ceiling like rain. His eyes grew used to the gloom and he heard a sound at the far end of one of the corridors, a great wrenching sound, the grinding of gears and the twisting of metal, as if a huge key was being turned in an enormous lock. Then there was a shaft of bright white light—daylight!—followed by a gust of fresh air. The low dungeon door in the base of the fortress walls had been thrown open. Ryan shrank back, hiding in the shadows, watching, praying—if there was only some way to get to that door . . .

The first thing he saw, though, made his heart sink down to his feet. A dozen or more Dragoon soldiers marched into the wide passageway, a phalanx of armed men, the plates of the armor on their chests touching as they marched side by side. It was a solid wall of steel and flesh that stood between Ryan and blessed freedom.

Then came a procession of figures in chains, villagers who had been rounded up by the soldiers and were now being muscled into slavery. Ryan recognized a couple of them, but none he knew by name until . . .

Ryan jumped to his feet and stared. In front of him stood Willy Beest and Mosely, the two huge Warmbloods being pushed through the fortress by a couple of Dragoon soldiers, who poked and prodded the captives with spears, moving these two reluctant prisoners down the corridor. There was a plan forming in Ryan's mind. Willy Beest and Mosely knew him, they knew that he was associated with Master Chung, and the five Warriors of Virtue. Would they help him escape? Would they risk their own skins to help a stranger? Ryan looked around, gazing back up the stairs. It was only a matter of time before every Dragoon soldier in the place was looking for him. He had to try to get away and he had to hope that Willy Beest and Mosely would come to his assistance.

Ryan got to his feet, abandoned his dark corner and stepped out into the middle of the passageway, allowing himself to be seen clearly. He hoped enough light penetrated.

Ryan filled his lungs with air. "Hey! How ya doin'?" he shouted as loud as he could.

For a moment, the soldiers stared at Ryan and Ryan could only stare back. Then they sprung into action.

"It's the Newcomer," yelled one of the Dragoon soldiers. "Seize him. Get him!"

But before any of the armed men could run toward Ryan, Ryan took off—and he was heading straight at them! And as he ran, he shouted at the top of his lungs: "Willy Beest! Mosely! Help me!"

Mosely and Willy Beest did not need another invitation. The big animals turned and slammed into guards, blocking for Ryan like two huge offensive linemen.

Ryan was right behind them, the Manuscript of Legend tucked under his arm like a football. The soldiers dove for him, but he high stepped out of their reach—he cut left, cut right and spun, dodging tacklers at every turn. Mosely and Willy Beest sailed through the air, slamming soldiers to the ground, leaving a pile of the men as Ryan leaped over them and blasted through the door and into the open air.

Ryan ran like he had never run before, thundering through the forest, the heavy Manuscript still clutched in his hands. He hurtled over fallen logs and ducked under low branches, running with skill and stealth. The elation of the escape passed in a moment. As he ran, he felt the pleasure begin to drain away, then a terrible despondency overcame him like a miserable, cold wave. He continued to run.

But as he ran, he began to cry, bitter tears pouring out his eyes. He was frightened and tired. Grief was crushing his chest as if an enormous weight had been placed on him. He had had enough . . .

A strong wind was blowing and Ryan found himself caught in a swirling cloud of dust and debris. He slowed to a stop—exhausted, overwhelmed and lost. He looked at the Manuscript in his hands, tears welling in his eyes and running down his cheeks. He threw the manuscript down on the ground, the wind whipping through the hundreds of blanks pages, and then he sat down, wedging himself into a crevice between two old, gnarled trees. Then Ryan put his head in his hands and cried.

His sobs wracked his body and his tears were hot and heartfelt. He had read the phrase, he had heard it countless times, but until that moment Ryan Jeffers had not realized that a heart really could be broken. Sorrow settled on him like a shroud, one that he felt he would never be able to shake off. "You didn't have to die," he wailed. "Why? Why did you do it, Elysia?"

A fresh, cold wave of grief broke over him. "And Master Chung . . . He's dead. He's *really dead*." Until now, death had always been an abstraction to him, not something that really happened to people—not people he knew. Death was something you heard about on the evening news or knew was just pretend, something in a movie or a television show. Now death was real.

"I don't want to see anymore," he said miserably. "I just don't want to see anymore . . ." He raised his eyes, looking into the dark trees above his head. "Mom! Where are you, Mom! *Mommy! Mom!* I don't want this. Why am I here? Take me home. I don't need it! Who put me here? Take me home! Please, someone take me home!" His distraught words, though, were snatched away by the swirling winds. No answer came.

It was too much for him to handle. He felt weak and spent, helpless to help himself. He wanted to be protected. All he wanted in that moment was just to be able to go back to being a kid again. Life in the real world had not been great, but it had not been filled with death and despair. "Help me!" Ryan shouted. "Please! Someone help me!"

But there was no response, no sound except the rushing of the wind. There was no one there to help him—except for Mudlap. The strange little creature seemed to have materialized out of the dirty, grit-filled wind. One moment he was not there, then the next he was.

"Will this help?"

Ryan looked up, startled by the sudden sound. Mudlap was standing in front of him holding Ryan's old watch out in front of him. The little fellow looked shy and contrite. He gestured with the watch, thrusting it ever closer to Ryan, as if the contraption was a sacred talisman that would solve all their problems, restore Tao to health and save them all from the force of evil that had wrought such destruction on the land.

"I don't know what this is," said Mudlap softly and slowly. "But if it will help you, you can have it back." This, of course, was a first. Mudlap was so greedy, so filled with avarice that he never returned anything—anything!—once he had it in the grasp of his little hands. But the destruction of the Lifespring, the death of Master Chung—these cataclysmic events had shown even him that some things were more valuable than mere possessions, some things were worth giving away if it meant that that the world could be reborn.

Ryan, of course, could not know this. Instead of being moved or touched, he just shot the little creature a nasty, withering glance, then turned away from him angrily.

"You stay away from me," he ordered. "I don't know much about this place. But I learned pretty quick that you are nothing but trouble. There's no way I'm going to start trusting you. Not now . . ." Ryan walked away, as if he knew where he was going. Then he stopped and Mudlap came running along on his stumpy legs, catching up to him.

"Why are you so sad, Newcomer?" Mudlap asked. There was genuine concern in his voice.

"Why am I sad?" Ryan asked, looking at Mudlap as if he was truly crazy. "What's the matter with you? Do I have to draw you a picture? Haven't you seen what's happened around here. Aren't *you* sad? Seems to me that Komodo isn't going to make your life any easier when he gets hold of you."

"Gets hold of me?" Mudlap squeaked. He

looked genuinely worried. "I haven't done anything to Lord Komodo."

"You haven't figured out you don't have to do anything," said Ryan bitterly. "Breathing is offensive enough. Komodo is going to get us all. You. Me. Everyone."

Mudlap did not look like he liked the sound of that at all. He held out the watch again. "Come on, take this thing back. Maybe it will make you feel a little better. Maybe you can use it to make everything better again. Maybe it has great powers. It makes noises from time to time, you know. Mysterious noises . . . Maybe it's trying to tell us something."

"Make me feel better?" Ryan snapped angrily. "A *watch*? Maybe it would make you feel better— but not me. All you care about is your stupid little things. Your *rewards*. You don't know what's important. Just leave me alone. Now, go away!"

But Ryan did not realize that Mudlap's feelings were absolutely genuine. He stared at Ryan softly, and it looked for a moment as if the little man might burst into tears himself. Instead, he snuffled a little bit and hopped on his feet nervously.

"I just want to help, that's all," Mudlap whined. "Why can't you believe that? I'm telling the truth, Newcomer. I really am." And he was. It was just that he had never told it before . . .

"I don't need your help," Ryan barked angrily.

"So why don't you just get out of here, you little creep."

Mudlap took a deep breath and turned away from Ryan. There were real tears in his eyes now. He started to walk away into the forest, looking small and insignificant among the tall, towering trees. But he had not gone far when he stopped and turned back.

"The Rooz need your help," he called out to the boy. "They are at the Temple Ruins. I thought you would want to know that." Then, summoning up as much dignity as he could muster, Mudlap walked away, vanishing into the dark and silent recesses of the forest.

THE ROOZ HAD FOUND MASTER CHUNG'S BODY WHERE HE had fallen. The horror they felt at seeing their master dead on the ground could not be allowed to overwhelm them. Master Chung had always taught them that they must learn to control their grief. Devastated though the five of them were— especially Yun—they dug a grave for Master Chung and reverently laid his body in the earth he had so revered during his long lifetime.

When they were done, they stood around the grave, as if at a holy shrine, all of them silent— their hopelessness and bereavement was far to great to be put into mere words. With the death of Master Chung all five of the Warriors of Virtue felt as if all had been lost, completely and irrevocably. Elysia's betrayal, the decimation of the village and the Lifespring, the enslavement of their friends—even Ryan was gone. It seemed that the day they had always dreaded, the terrible end, had finally come.

But the death of Master Chung was the greatest burden to bear. He had done more for them than anyone, had given them as much life as their own parents had. He had taught them, molded them, created them. Without him they would never have found the keys to the powers they possessed, the strengths and virtues locked so deep inside them, inside every person.

Yes, truly the end had come.

Or had it?

Yee sensed it first. As he gazed at the grave, a mere mound of close-packed earth—nothing like the memorial Master Chung deserved—he became aware of a scent on the breeze. He raised his nose and sniffed tentatively, his ears perking up as he did so.

Then Tsun sensed it. Then Chi. Then all five of them turned and saw Ryan standing behind them, the Manuscript clutched in his hands. Instantly their spirits lifted. It was a miracle. One of them had escaped from the clutches of Komodo, and if one had, maybe others had . . . Maybe there was hope after all, maybe the fight was not over.

"Ryan!" Tsun cried.

"We thought you were dead!" Lai shouted.

"Thank goodness you're alive," said Chi.

Seeing Ryan even made Yee and Yun try to climb out of the depths of their grief.

But Ryan's black despair still had him tight in its grips. He could not share their elation. His face was solemn and the Rooz realized that something was wrong. Ryan looked at all of them, his eyes still wet with his hot, sorrowful tears.

"I cannot help you," Ryan said sadly. "I wish I could. I tried. I really tried. But I can't."

The five Warriors stared back at him with questioning looks on their faces, wondering at his words. There was such sorrow in his voice that they knew that there had to be more, that he would tell them more, something he knew that they did not. And that he was going to say something deadly serious.

Ryan opened the Manuscript of Legend and showed the blank pages to the five Rooz.

"I tried to read it," he said. "It's empty. There's nothing written here. Nothing. I'm sorry . . ."

Ryan backed away from his friends, feeling like the smallest person in the world. The Rooz too, so elated just moments before, had descended once again into despondency, their world in tatters once again. And, Ryan thought miserably, it was all his fault.

17

THE LIFESPRING WAS DYING QUICKLY. THE BEAUTIFUL waterfall had dried up, silenced in the dead and decaying landscape. Dry, lifeless sand had replaced the crystal water of the lake. A broken waterwheel from the old mill lay on the shoreline; the mill itself was in ruins. Lifeless trees and other vegetation heeled over at odd angles, their dead roots half pulled from the ground. The bridges and pathways were wrecked beyond repair, the platforms broken down, the huts and houses smoking ruins. A sharp wind blew sand and grit through the village, choking and evil-smelling, as if death and destruction could be carried on the air.

Among this chaos were hundreds of Dragoon soldiers—all of them in a general state of hysteria—searching through the rubble. They looked under the demolished Council Round, behind the broken waterwheel, along the platforms and walkways, looking for any sign of the Rooz, Ryan or the precious Manuscript. They found nothing.

General Grillo was in charge, watching over his men with a look of profound panic on his face. Komodo was angrier and more out of control than Grillo had ever seen him—there was no telling what he would do if General Grillo and his soldiers did not deliver their quarry to him. Grillo knew that he himself was teetering on the edge of a very long and painful death. There was no flight—there was no place to hide.

Dullard and Mantose were there too, but they did not seem to be worried about anything. Neither did they seem to miss their erstwhile partner-in-murder Barbra-Rotious. She was gone and that meant all the more attention from the Lord Komodo for the two of them. Not to mention that this pair of twisted killers seemed to be enjoying the panic and confusion that had spread through the last serene, good place in Tao.

"Marinade in wisdom. Simmer in righteousness!" Mantose shrieked, capering wildly about like a madman. "Tiny little pieces! Find them! Chop! Chop! Chop!"

Pacing back and forth, fighting down his own panic, Grillo tried to ignore the two nasty creatures. Let these little lunatics enjoy the destruction while they could.

The Manuscript of Legend had to be found. The Newcomer had to be found also. The Rooz had to be destroyed once and for all.

There was absolutely no telling what Komodo would do if these plans were not carried out. It was of the utmost importance. It was not revenge, it was not a desire to win. It was far more momentous than anything like that.

Grillo knew, as no one else knew, that Komodo needed the Manuscript and the Newcomer to go on living. Somehow Komodo had divined that the Manuscript could transport him to another world—perhaps the world the Newcomer had fled—and once there he could begin again to reconstruct his empire of evil. Grillo knew Komodo well enough to know that the Lord would not hesitate to sacrifice anyone or anything if it meant that he himself could have his own life continue.

A gust of wind swirled through the chaotic scene, a blast of foul air thick with dust and debris. And out of it stepped Komodo himself. He climbed up onto the Council Round, seated himself in the chair that Master Chung had always sat in and looked around.

No one quite noticed him at first. Komodo was annoyed at Dullard and Mantose—their manic ranting echoed above the scene. Komodo looked at them hard, as if putting them in his sights, and suddenly the two psychopaths flew off the platform and tumbled to the sand bed of the lake. Astonished, they got to their feet, spitting sand from their mouths.

Grillo saw them fall, then he caught sight of Komodo and his heart sank.

"General Grillo," said Komodo, snapping his fingers. "The Manuscript if you please."

Grillo gulped. "We have searched everywhere, my lord. We cannot find the Manuscript."

Komodo nodded. "I'm curious, General, has your search taken you to where it actually is, by any chance?"

Grillo's shoulders slumped a little more. "I'm sorry, my lord," he whispered.

Komodo ignored the apology. It was as if he had not even heard it. "And are you so stupid as to think that they would hide it here?" He jumped to his feet and glared at his incompetent general and at his bumbling soldiers. "Get out of here! All of you! I want you to search in every direction until that Manuscript is found!"

"Go!" Grillo bellowed.

Like frightened children, the soldiers and lieutenants swarmed through the pathways leading out of the Lifespring. Grillo bowed to Komodo in compliance, then quickly hurried after his troops.

The Lifespring was in total chaos. Leaves, dust and other debris swirled around Komodo like a hurricane. But in the spot where Komodo was sitting, all was calm. He was in the eye of the storm—he *was* the eye of the storm, a storm that he himself had created. He leaned back in Master Chung's chair and closed his eyes. He smiled to himself and looked rather serene, despite the discord and destruction around him. Victory was coming. He knew it was out there, he could taste it on the bitter wind.

SOMETHING HAD STIRRED IN THE ROOZ AS WELL. CHI HAD examined the Manuscript, glancing at the blank pages in despair. There was nothing to be gained from these pieces of blank paper . . . Maybe, if Master Chung had been alive, they could have made sense of it. He shook his head slowly. One by one, they glanced at each other. Their dark eyes all telegraphed the same unspoken message: *What is to be done?*

It was Yee who rallied them wordlessly. His hands fluttered in a flurry of sign gestures.

Lai nodded as he read the hand movements. "Yee is absolute right. This is our home."

Ryan looked on, distressed at what the Rooz were contemplating. It was certain death.

Lai stepped up to Yun. From under his robe he pulled a sword. Yun's beautiful crystalline sword. He handed it over to Yun, who took it reverently in his hands.

"Live . . . or die," Lai said. "That is the choice."

Yun looked at the mighty sword in his hands. Then he looked at his fellow warriors. "Why not?" he said simply.

KOMODO REMAINED ON MASTER CHUNG'S THRONE. Beyond him, the sand and leaves continued to swirl through the deserted Lifespring. His eyes were closed, as if he were lost in deep meditation. But a noise made him open his eyes, a beautiful noise. It was a series of high, wispy notes played on a slight wooden flute, a gentle melody that carried through the trees, over the ruins, along the bridges, down the pathway . . .

Komodo opened his eyes. Standing on one of the bridges facing him were the five Warriors of Virtue. Yun was in the middle, armed with his sword, ready for battle, the others flanking him. They looked equally resolute and ready for the fight.

Komodo beamed, looking absolutely delighted at the sudden arrival of these unexpected visitors. He held his arms out wide, a gesture of warm welcome for the Rooz.

"Oh, Warriors," Komodo shouted joyously. "So good of you to come out and play!"

"You have come uninvited into our Lifespring, Komodo," Yun proclaimed solemnly. "You have done damage here. You have invaded our home. We want it back."

Komodo laughed heartily, seeming to really enjoy the joke. "Oh, but you don't understand . . . Virtue has been forgotten, Yun. And I have taken its place! So do as you wish!"

Then Komodo flew directly up into the air, vanishing into the thicket of branches. The Rooz craned their necks looking for him, but it seemed as if Komodo had disappeared completely.

When he became visible again, he was diving like a bomb at the base of the bridge, his massive sword clutched in his hands. Komodo swung it in an arc as he passed, aiming for Yun's head, but Yun jumped, dodging the blow. The Rooz scattered as the sword split the bridge's supports, cutting them clean in half, the splintered timbers raining down on Komodo. There was an explosion of dust and he rose from the rubble, bellowing like a madman, his eyes demonic.

Yun landed on the waterwheel, the crystalline sword in his hand, the other Rooz on either side. Komodo raised his arms, his teeth clenched tightly, eyes closed, a look of utter insanity on his face. Suddenly, there were two more Komodos! Two figures bursting out of his taut body, then two more emerging from the first two. Komodo had harnessed his Kung so completely that he could manifest himself several times over—there was more than enough evil in his heart to go around. Now five Komodos faced the five Warriors of Virtue in mortal combat.

Each Komodo took a step forward, thrusting out his hands, sending spears of red fire blasting toward the Rooz, throwing them back. Through the chaos the wind picked up, a whirlwind of leaves and debris.

All at once the five Komodos became hard missiles of sand and fire, shooting out at the Rooz. One flew at Yun still balanced on the waterwheel. Another shot at Chi, who stood on a corner bridge. Another went for Yee on the high bridge. Yet another raced toward Tsun, who stood on the remains of the Council Round, while the last shot toward Lai, who stood on the ground in front of the broken bridge.

Yun barely had time to react as the Komodo missile bore down on him. He raised his sword quickly, blocking a lance blow with a thunderous clash of weapons. The two warriors spun off each other, exchanging powerful, punishing blows.

Suddenly, the waterwheel began to roll toward the bridge, Yun and Komodo treading the wheel as they fought—it was all they could do to keep their balance.

"Can you stop cruelty, Yun?" Komodo snarled.

"I am cruelty. And I am ready to kill again. Are you?"

Yun did not answer. He blocked another swipe by Komodo. Suddenly Komodo twirled himself up and into the air, dropping out of sight in the blink of an eye. Yun continued to tread the waterwheel, but he was alone there, his head swiveling as he looked for Komodo.

He found him. He was inside the wheel itself, jabbing his lance up through the wood as Yun and the wheel continued to roll. With each jab, Yun leaped into the air, the lance missing him by inches, splinters flying like bullets. Komodo jabbed again and again, but Yun had no way of counterattacking. If he lost his timing or his footing for even a moment, he would be thrown in front of the heavy wheel and crushed.

Yee was engaged in a fierce battle of his own, with his own copy of Komodo. Komodo lashed out with the lance, but Yee caught it with his metal ring, sparks flying as steel bit into steel. Yee double backflipped away from his attacker, but he did not get far away enough. Fire sprouted from the tip of the lance, the heat so intense that it melted some of the metal pieces on Yee's tunic and belt. Komodo cackled and grinned, immensely enjoying this part of the deadly game.

"Still nothing to say?" he asked, laughing wildly. "Then I will be your voice, Yee."

Yee somersaulted off the bridge, grabbed hold

of a rope hanging from the ruins and swung to the other side, Komodo following suit, right behind him, shrieking with laughter.

Lai pulled himself through the trees, branch to branch, with the sureness of a monkey, dodging a series of bone-crushing blows from yet another copy of Komodo. Then Komodo grabbed one of the vines hanging from the upper boughs and swung round the tree as if playing a giant, deadly game of tetherball, coming around the stout trunk and slamming into Lai from the rear. Lai tumbled, falling through the tree limbs to the ground. He hit and jumped to his feet, wielding his wooden staff. But Komodo's metal lance was a far more potent, lethal piece of weaponry.

They smashed against each other, the powerful lance chopping through the staff, whacking it down, piece by piece. In a matter of seconds, Lai had nothing in his hands but a tiny stub. The two fighters squared off, each holding out his weapon—Lai was seriously overmatched. Komodo grinned broadly.

"Things fall apart, Lai," Komodo screamed. "The center cannot hold. And that means *chaos*!"

Then he pounced on Lai, coming at him, charging forward, unleashing a furious barrage of kicks and jabs.

No sooner had Chi produced his flaming whips, coils of wild flame writhing in the air, than his version of Komodo generated blazing whips of his own: Their straps and lashes intertwining, setting off a fireworks display that lit up the forest.

"You are just an illusion, Komodo!" Chi taunted his opponent. "You do not exist!" Chi used his two whips to snag a piece of the bridge above his head, yanking hard and propelling himself into the air, just missing a fatal blow from Komodo. Komodo tossed aside his whips, and his lance appeared in his hand. He brought it down, slashing wildly.

Tsun and Komodo circled each other. He grinned at her, mocking and winking, blowing little kisses in her direction. He seemed to have changed form slightly, becoming a curvy and effeminate version of himself, preening, showing off his own beauty.

"I find beauty far more attractive," he declared prissily. "Enough of all this nasty fighting!"

But Tsun had not had enough. She leaped into the air and tried to swat Komodo with her powerful tail. But she was not fast enough—Komodo grabbed her tail and slammed her against the wall. Tsun slumped and fell as Komodo smashed her off the walls of the Council Round and she tumbled with a tremendous crash.

Yun was still on the waterwheel. Komodo continued to jab his lance up through the wooden planks, just missing Yun with each ferocious thrust. Yun finally found his timing, leaping to avoid a shot but coming down with his sword at the ready. But as the mighty sword cut through the wood, splintering it, Komodo simply vanished, gone before the blade reached him.

Lai was in the trees again, leaping through the branches. Komodo chased him, spinning around, but becoming dizzy as he tried to keep up. As Lai turned to attack, mustering all the force he could—*whoosh!*—Komodo disappeared. Lai smashed into the tree trunk, sending up a great explosion of wood and bark and branches.

Chi used his whips to twirl around and around the arch of the bridge like a gymnast. When he let go, he somersaulted, igniting his whips again as he spun, but just as he was about to come down on Komodo, this one was gone as well. The twirling whips wrapped around Chi instead, exploding in a profusion of sparks and flame.

Tsun had turned on Komodo, her strength and grace battling him back. But when she was ready to press the advantage—Komodo was gone, vanishing into thin air . . .

Komodo could not be seen, but his presence could be felt as the Rooz stumbled around, bewildered by Komodo's strange, supernatural behavior. He left behind him, a tornado of sand, leaves and broken pieces from the many structures. The whirlwind was stronger than anything they had felt, a force of nature that seemed to have an animal malice bred into it.

The Rooz were blown off their feet by the wind and were buried under chunks of debris as a thunderous roar drowned out every sound. A noise so loud that it caused pain, slicing through the middle of their heads, confusing their thoughts, weakening them further . . .

RYAN SAT ALONE NEXT TO MASTER CHUNG'S GRAVE WITH the Manuscript of Legend on his lap. He had it open, but the pages were still blank. He flipped through them one more time, hoping this time he might see something, the slightest mark, that would unlock the secret of the enigmatic book. But it was as it had always been. Nothing.

Tears welled in his eyes and he looked up at the sky, wondering if that was where you went when you died. Because he was convinced now that he was doomed. If Komodo could slay a man like Master Chung, then what chance did a puny kid like Ryan have against such power?

"Mom, Dad," Ryan whispered softly. "I won't ever see you again . . . I'm sorry."

A tear rolled down his cheek and dropped onto the open page of the Manuscript. Ryan glanced down . . . And saw something. He wiped the little drop of salty liquid off the page. He studied it closely for a moment or two, the look on his face changing from sorrow, to hope, to awe. He snapped the book shut, got to his feet and ran.

18

THE WIND OF DEBRIS HAD DIED DOWN IN THE LIFESPRING.
All was quiet. Komodo was nowhere to be seen.
Yun lay hurt on the ground, the other Rooz
gathering around him. They were all scarred and
beaten, but Yun had suffered more than the
others.

"Yun?" Lai asked. "Are you all right?"

Yun did not answer, but he got to his feet,
wincing in pain as he did so. His eyes were
locked on something behind the other Rooz. He
was pale, as if he had seen a ghost.

In fact, he had.

Standing near the broken bridge was the figure

of Master Chung, his image spiritual and radiant. The other Rooz followed the line of Yun's gaze and turned to see the apparition.

"Master Chung!" Lai said, his voice hushed and low.

Yun took a step toward the phantom, advancing with a sad, guilt-ridden look on his face.

"Master Chung," he said with a respectful bow.

Master Chung shook his head slowly and looked as if he were disappointed in his star pupil. "Yun, why didn't you listen to me? You acted in such haste. Now the Lifespring is gone."

Yun was near tears and he bowed his head in supplication. "Master . . . ," he said, his voice choked with emotion. "I have failed you. Please. Please, tell me what to do now."

Master Chung smiled a kindly smile and stepped forward, putting a hand on Yun's shoulder, a warm, reassuring, fatherly gesture. Yun seemed to relax a little, as if he had been forgiven.

Then Master Chung's hand closed around Yun's throat, squeezing hard, choking the life out of him. As the other Warriors jumped back, shocked and stunned at what had happened, there was a flash of smoke and a blast of wind and Master Chung metamorphosed into Komodo!

"Tell you what to do?" Komodo snarled. "I'll tell you want to do. You can go to hell!"

Yun had let his guard down completely and he

was powerless to fight for his life. With the strength of a giant, Komodo lifted the Roo warrior off his feet, holding him in the air, as if his right arm were the cross beam of a gallows. Yun writhed and gasped, as the life was squeezed out of him.

"Hey! Komodo! Looking for this?" Ryan was standing on the pile of rubble that had once been the Council Round, the Manuscript of Legend in his hands.

"Hey . . . Remember me?" Ryan continued. "I'm your friend! And I'm proud to be your destiny. Like this book . . . Of course, I can't read it. So what good is it to me." Casually, he ripped a page from the book, balled it up and threw it over his shoulder. Then he grabbed another one. The sound of tearing paper seemed to fill the clearing.

"Nooooo!" screamed Komodo. He threw Yun into the other Rooz, knocking them backward. Then he leaped into the air with a tremendous yell, swooping after Ryan, who dove for the cover of Master Chung's half-shattered throne.

"Chi, *five is one!* Positive Kung!" Ryan yelled urgently. "Do it now! *Now!*"

Komodo dove for Ryan, his arm sweeping back, absorbing all the energy he could muster and delivering a tremendous blast of Negative Kung. Ryan threw himself to the ground, but the blast hit him in the leg. The force of impact was like thunder, catapulting him into the air. Master Chung's throne exploded, turning to gravel in an instant.

Komodo was on the ground, exhausted by the exertions. He fought to draw a single, weak breath as he scrabbled in the debris, looking for the torn pages of the Manuscript.

"No, no, no," he moaned as he crawled in the rubble. "It cannot be destroyed." Something made him turn, and he saw Chi raise his medallion, watched the other four medallions rise up to meet the first, felt almost transfixed by the mingling of fire, metal, earth, wood, and water. Komodo could feel the power of Elements and Virtues surging through the medallions, but he wasn't prepared for what happened next. The Rooz somehow joined together, forming a powerful vortex of energy—that was aimed right at him. They smashed into him like a tornado, moving through his body from his head down to his toes. They were inside him, cleaning the evil that had so long stained his soul and his heart.

Komodo's body convulsed from the impact. He opened his mouth and screamed in agony as the embodiment of virtue that had once been the Rooz exploded from his body, millions of bright white lights shooting out in every direction. Komodo's body erupted, a great white flash, brighter than the sun that turned the black night into bright day.

Then, as the light faded, there came silence. Yun, Chi, Lai and Tsun stood there, rising up from the debris. All that seemed to remain of Komodo—his cape—lay rumpled on the ground. The Rooz looked at one another in disbelief, not quite able to believe that Komodo had been defeated at long last.

Tsun spoke first. "Where's Yee? And where's Ryan?" she asked.

Yee stepped forward, Ryan stretched in his strong arms. The boy's eyes were closed, his head drooping. Very gently, Yee set him down on the ground, the other Rooz gathering around him.

"Ryan?" said Tsun.

His eyes opened, but his look was unfocused, almost as if he was seeing a dream. "Did . . . did it work?" he asked.

Chi nodded and revealed a page from the Manuscript, the one Ryan had deciphered with his tears. At first, they could only see the words "Positive Kung" and "Negative Kung," a mirror image of each other. But then, for a fleeting moment, a few simple words danced on the page, the wisdom of the Manuscript of Legend: *"When you take a life, you lose a part of yourself."* Then the image faded away, leaving the page pristine and blank.

"Komodo expended all his energy when he tried to kill Ryan with Negative Kung," he explained. "It weakened him enough—he could not withstand all five of us. Ryan saved us all . . ."

Tsun touched Ryan softly, a look of profound pride and gratitude on her face. But then there was more commotion. The Dragoon soldiers were swarming back into the village. They were armed and ready to fight.

"Oh no," Yun groaned.

Grillo was at the head of his troops. He and Yun stared at each other for a moment.

"Grillo," said Yun. "It is over. Join us in peace."

Before Grillo could respond, they all heard a small, weak voice.

"Water . . . anyone? Please . . . I am so thirsty. Please, could someone help me?"

It was Komodo, trapped among the rubble of the broken bridge. It looked like Komodo—but it was a different sort of man. The evil had been wiped from his face; his eyes were soft and gentle.

Grillo stepped over to him and looked at him closely. Komodo stared up with innocence in his eyes. "I'm lost," he said. "Please, would someone take me home?"

Grillo did not know how to react, but Yun did. He stepped up, looking at Komodo kindly.

"This is your home, my friend," he said.

As Grillo took off his helmet and dropped his sword, his soldiers started to come forward, one by one, to offer up their arms. Even Dullard and Mantose, once they had gotten a peek at their former overlord, as helpless as a baby on the ground, gave up their weapons and surrendered. Grillo stripped off his cloak and wrapped it around Komodo's shoulders.

There had been a time when there was a boy named Ryan Jeffers who would have thought that Komodo did not deserve this kind of treatment, who would have thought that the body of Komodo should be punished for all the evil he had created, all the pain he had caused, even though it was evil and pain born in a mind that no longer existed. The kind treatment of this new man would not have been satisfying to that Ryan Jeffers—this was not the good guys beating the bad guys.

But that Ryan Jeffers had ceased to exist. The new Ryan Jeffers had learned, under the tutelage of Master Chung and by the example of the Rooz, that the positive side of nature will always win out, that forgiveness is a virtue of Positive Kung.

Ryan suddenly understood. All the things that had mattered in his life up till then did not matter. His leg did not matter. Glory on the football field did not matter. Hanging with the right kids—none of it mattered. Not if your spirit was pure, your path the path of virtue.

Yee extended his hand to Ryan and the two exchanged a weak version of their special handshake. Yee smiled, then spoke his first words in a long, long time. His words came out slow and gentle.

"Thank you," he said softly. "Thank you, Ryan."

19

"RYAN! *IN OR OUT!*"

He was back in the water treatment station and Brad was taunting him, daring him to risk his life to gain something as fleeting and insubstantial as acceptance in a clique.

Ryan was supposed to take that last fateful step all over again, but this time his foot stopped in midair. He glanced down at his leg—same old leg—in fact everything was the same, exactly as it had been before the water threw him off the pipes.

Everything was the same, except for Ryan. A smile crept across his face, a smile of confidence, of pride. He glanced at Brad, then looked at the rest of them, confusing them with the odd grin on his face.

"Ryan, let's get out of here!" Chucky yelled.

Ryan nodded. "Why not?" He walked back to safety, stopping next to Tracy and Chucky, both of whom were puzzled and surprised by this sudden change of behavior.

But no one was more amazed than Brad. "Hey! Where do you think you're going?"

"Finally the man's come to his senses."

Ryan smiled at Chucky and winked. "We've got a lot to talk about." He looked around the dank chamber. It looked too much like other such rooms he had been in recently "But somewhere else, I think." He started toward the metal ladder.

"Jeffers!" yelled Brad, his voice loud and irate. "You limp dick! You didn't make the cut! You'll never make the cut, pansy ass!"

"Shut up, Brad," Tracy snapped. Was she the only one who could appreciate the strength it had taken *not* to go with the pack?

"Save it!"

"That's it," said Tracy. "I am outta here." She ran down the shaft and caught up with Ryan, who was standing next to the ladder, waiting for Chucky to go up first. He stepped aside gallantly, gesturing that Tracy should go first. They shared a knowing smile.

"Tracy!" Brad screamed. "Get back here! You're gonna—"

But the rest of his words were drowned out by the rumbling deep in the walls. The concrete walls began to tremble and all the kids looked around, frightened at what was going to happen next.

Suddenly, a torrent of water exploded out of the spillway, a great eruption that washed through the room, smashing the pipes that stretched across the void to the ledge where Brad stood alone. He was screaming and crying, terrified that he had been stranded—between him and safety was a really deep pool of filthy water.

"What are you looking at, you miscarriages!" Brad shrieked. "Come on, get me out of here. *Do something!*"

Chucky raised an eyebrow and glanced at Ryan. "Think we ought to call 911?"

"Oh definitely," said Ryan. "In a while . . ."

RYAN WAS IN BED—HIS OWN, WARM, SAFE, COMFORTABLE bed—his trusty dog Bravo next to him, when he heard his mother's car pull into the driveway. A few moments later the door to his bedroom opened.

"Ryan?" his mother called into the darkness. "Are you asleep?"

Ryan snapped on his bedside light. "No. Not really."

"Hi," his mom said. "How was your night?"

"Virtuous," said Ryan.

Kathryn wasn't quite sure what to make of that, but took it to be a good thing. "Really?"

"Really," Ryan replied with a smile. "So, how many houses did you sell today, Mom?"

"Oh . . . at least a dozen," she said. "Good night, honey." She started to close the door behind her. But Ryan called her back.

"Mom?"

"Yes?"

"I love you."

That was not quite what she was expecting. But she was touched and a warm smile broke across her face.

"I love you too . . . Good night."

She closed the door behind her but paused on the threshold for a moment. She worried about her son so much, worried that his disability held him back, made him stand out . . . but in her heart she knew that Ryan was fine. He was just fine.

Bravo's nose twitched and he lifted his head, looking toward the window. Ryan felt the movement and sat up, his own eyes drawn to the window. Sitting on the sill was the jar containing Ming's cocoon.

"I don't believe it," Ryan whispered aloud. He grabbed the jar and unscrewed the cap and

found a note stuck to the underside. He un-
wrapped it and read it in the faint light.

"'Spread your wings, Ryan,'" he whispered.

There was still a thunderstorm on the horizon,
but there was something in that rumble. A voice
and it was a voice Ryan recognized . . . It was
the voice of Yee.

"Thank . . . you . . . ," the voice whispered
softly.

Ryan's eyes went wide and he turned to Bravo,
who was looking at him curiously.

"Bravo . . . ," Ryan whispered. "It was real?
Could it have been real? Did it really happen to
me?"

Then Bravo did a most curious thing—without being asked, he raised a paw to shake Ryan's
hand. Ryan smiled and did his over/under shake,
the same handshake he'd done with Yee.

Bravo tilted his head, and in the moonlight
streaming through the window, the dog's face
looked remarkably like that of a Roo Warrior . . .